W9-AVE-374

# THE FORTUNES OF TEXAS

## SHIPMENT 1

*Healing Dr. Fortune* by Judy Duarte
*Mendoza's Return* by Susan Crosby
*Fortune's Just Desserts* by Marie Ferrarella
*Fortune's Secret Baby* by Christyne Butler
*Fortune Found* by Victoria Pade
*Fortune's Cinderella* by Karen Templeton

## SHIPMENT 2

*Fortune's Valentine Bride* by Marie Ferrarella
*Mendoza's Miracle* by Judy Duarte
*Fortune's Hero* by Susan Crosby
*Fortune's Unexpected Groom* by Nancy Robards Thompson
*Fortune's Perfect Match* by Allison Leigh
*Her New Year's Fortune* by Allison Leigh

## SHIPMENT 3

*A Date with Fortune* by Susan Crosby
*A Small Fortune* by Marie Ferrarella
*Marry Me, Mendoza!* by Judy Duarte
*Expecting Fortune's Heir* by Cindy Kirk
*A Change of Fortune* by Crystal Green
*Happy New Year, Baby Fortune!* by Leanne Banks
*A Sweetheart for Jude Fortune* by Cindy Kirk

## SHIPMENT 4

*Lassoed by Fortune* by Marie Ferrarella
*A House Full of Fortunes!* by Judy Duarte
*Falling for Fortune* by Nancy Robards Thompson
*Fortune's Prince* by Allison Leigh
*A Royal Fortune* by Judy Duarte
*Fortune's Little Heartbreaker* by Cindy Kirk

## SHIPMENT 5

*Mendoza's Secret Fortune* by Marie Ferrarella
*The Taming of Delaney Fortune* by Michelle Major
*My Fair Fortune* by Nancy Robards Thompson
*Fortune's June Bride* by Allison Leigh
*Plain Jane and the Playboy* by Marie Ferrarella
*Valentine's Fortune* by Allison Leigh

## SHIPMENT 6

*Triple Trouble* by Lois Faye Dyer
*Fortune's Woman* by RaeAnne Thayne
*A Fortune Wedding* by Kristin Hardy
*Her Good Fortune* by Marie Ferrarella
*A Tycoon in Texas* by Crystal Green
*In a Texas Minute* by Stella Bagwell

## SHIPMENT 7

*Cowboy at Midnight* by Ann Major
*A Baby Changes Everything* by Marie Ferrarella
*In the Arms of the Law* by Peggy Moreland
*Lone Star Rancher* by Laurie Paige
*The Good Doctor* by Karen Rose Smith
*The Debutante* by Elizabeth Bevarly

## SHIPMENT 8

*Keeping Her Safe* by Myrna Mackenzie
*The Law of Attraction* by Kristi Gold
*Once a Rebel* by Sheri WhiteFeather
*Military Man* by Marie Ferrarella
*Fortune's Legacy* by Maureen Child
*The Reckoning* by Christie Ridgway

THE **FORTUNES** OF **TEXAS**

# FALLING
# FOR FORTUNE

*Nancy Robards Thompson*

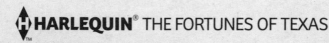

**HARLEQUIN**® THE FORTUNES OF TEXAS

If you purchased this book without a cover you should be aware that this book is stolen property. It was reported as "unsold and destroyed" to the publisher, and neither the author nor the publisher has received any payment for this "stripped book."

Special thanks and acknowledgment are given to Nancy Robards Thompson for her contribution to the Fortunes of Texas: Welcome to Horseback Hollow continuity.

Recycling programs for this product may not exist in your area.

ISBN-13: 978-1-335-68055-6

Falling for Fortune

Copyright © 2014 by Harlequin Books S.A.

All rights reserved. Except for use in any review, the reproduction or utilization of this work in whole or in part in any form by any electronic, mechanical or other means, now known or hereafter invented, including xerography, photocopying and recording, or in any information storage or retrieval system, is forbidden without the written permission of the publisher, Harlequin Enterprises Limited, 22 Adelaide St. West, 40th Floor, Toronto, Ontario M5H 4E3, Canada.

This is a work of fiction. Names, characters, places and incidents are either the product of the author's imagination or are used fictitiously, and any resemblance to actual persons, living or dead, business establishments, events or locales is entirely coincidental.

This edition published by arrangement with Harlequin Books S.A.

For questions and comments about the quality of this book, please contact us at CustomerService@Harlequin.com.

® and TM are trademarks of Harlequin Enterprises Limited or its corporate affiliates. Trademarks indicated with ® are registered in the United States Patent and Trademark Office, the Canadian Intellectual Property Office and in other countries.

**Printed in U.S.A.**

www.Harlequin.com

National bestselling author **Nancy Robards Thompson** holds a degree in journalism. She worked as a newspaper reporter until she realized reporting "just the facts" bored her silly. Now that she has much more content to report to her muse, Nancy loves writing women's fiction and romance full-time. Critics have deemed her work "funny, smart and observant." She resides in Florida with her husband and daughter. You can reach her at nancyrobardsthompson.com and Facebook.com/nancyrobardsthompsonbooks.

This book is dedicated to the memory of my sweet mother-in-law, Juanita Eitreim. I miss you every day.

# Chapter 1

"I'm sorry, sir, I've checked the directory three times. There's nobody by that name listed."

Strains of the new receptionist's voice carried in through Christopher Fortune's partially open door. He looked up from his in-office putting green.

What was her name again? He couldn't remember. It was only the start of her second week. Jeez, but she was shrill. He'd have to talk to her about her tone. Not good for community relations. But first...

He realigned his stance as the golf pro had taught him, making sure that his toes were parallel to the pin at the end of the fourteen-foot portable green. He set the putter in the hollow part of his left hand and placed the right hand so that his right thumb rested on the left side of the shaft. He pulled back to take his shot—

"Sir, I don't know what else to tell you." Now her voice was teetering on exasperation. He couldn't hear what the other person was saying, but she was giving him a headache. "We have a Christopher Fortune, but nobody by the name of *Chris Jones* works here. Could he be the one you're looking for?"

The words made Christopher hit the ball a little too hard. It rolled off the end of the green and under the coffee table that was part of the furniture grouping at the end of the room.

Who was asking for Chris Jones?

Two months ago, Chris Jones had adopted his mother's Fortune family name and moved to Red Rock from Horseback Hollow, Texas. He'd dropped the Jones portion of his name when he'd accepted the new job. Now, he was Christopher Fortune, vice president in charge of community relations for the Fortune Foundation.

Christopher set down his putter, walked over and fully opened his office door to see what the ruckus was about.

*What the hell—*

"Toby?" Christopher said flatly when he saw his brother and his new sister-in-law, Angie, standing there. "What are you doing here, man?"

The receptionist, a slight woman with close-cropped black hair, looked so young that she could've easily been mistaken for a sixteen-year-old. She turned and froze, all wide dark eyes and pale skin, when she saw Christopher.

"Oh! I'm sorry, Mr. Fortune. I didn't understand that they were looking for you. They asked for Chris Jones."

Now she was blushing.

Christopher glanced at the name plate that was front and center on the reception desk.

"Don't worry about it, Beverly. It's fine."

"Hey, little brother," Toby said, extending a hand. "Good to see you."

Christopher shook Toby's hand. His brother immediately pulled him into an awkward hold that their sister, Stacey, was fond of calling a *man hug:* a greeting that started as a handshake and ended with the guys leaning in and stiffly slapping each other on the back a couple of times.

When they broke apart, Christopher stepped back, reclaiming his dignity just in time to see both elevator doors open and Kinsley Aaron, the Foundation's outreach coordinator, step into the reception area.

Her long, straight blond hair hung loose around her shoulders, framing her pretty face. God, she was gorgeous, even if she was a little too uptight for his taste. He straightened his tie and raked his fingers through his hair, trying to right what Toby's enthusiastic bear hug had mussed.

Kinsley had the bluest eyes he'd ever seen. Those eyes were two of the reasons he always remembered her name. Although, the dowdy way she dressed wasn't much of an enticement. He couldn't figure out why such a beauty chose to dress like a schoolmarm. She always covered up as much of herself as possible. Didn't she know her modesty only made him daydream about the gifts that were undoubtedly hidden beneath all that wrapping?

As Kinsley approached Beverly's desk, she arched a brow at him. For a split second he could've sworn she'd read his mind. But he knew it was a ridiculous thought. She was probably just curious about Toby and Angie, since she tended to take her job so seriously. After all, this was an office where visitors generally came seeking help, something that typically fell into her community outreach division.

Before Kinsley could start asking questions, Christopher turned to his brother and sister-in-law. "Why don't we go into my office? We can talk in there."

He made quick work of ushering them out of the reception area. This sure as hell wasn't the most ideal time or place for a family reunion. Especially when he was determined to keep his life in Horseback Hollow worlds apart from the new life he'd created for himself in Red Rock.

Before he shut the door, he cast one last glance back at Kinsley, who was still lingering by Bev's desk. They locked gazes, and Christopher felt that old familiar *zing* that always happened when he looked into those eyes. The virtual vibration lasted even after she looked away.

And she was always the first one to look away.

He was pondering that when Toby said, "Since you were too darned busy to come home for the wedding, I decided I'd bring my beautiful bride to see you. Angie, you've met Chris before. Chris, this is my wife. Can you believe it?" he said, grinning. "I have a wife."

"Good to see you again, Angie," Christopher said, keeping his tone all business and shaking Angie's hand.

"So, they call you *Mr. Fortune* around here?" Toby asked, a note of good-natured ribbing in his voice. But before Christopher could answer, Toby let loose a low whistle as he glanced around Christopher's new digs. "Would you look at this fancy place? I guess you're doing all right for yourself, little brother."

"It's a pretty sweet gig," Christopher said. "Actually, I wanted to work directly for Uncle James at JMF Financial, but how could I argue after I found out that he'd created a position just for me? I'm sure he could do something for you if you want. All you have to do is ask."

What Christopher didn't say was that the work was a little boring and "do-gooder" for his taste. But the salary they were paying him, which was commensurate with the Fortune name rather than his experience, more than made up for the lack of excitement.

If Christopher had learned one thing over the past two months it was that he had to create his own excitement, ensure his own future. It wasn't as if he'd been blazing trails in Horseback Hollow. Nope, back home, he'd been bored and broke.

And a nobody.

Now he had a job that people respected and the bank account to go with it. So he figured why not go for the trifecta and take on the Fortune name? It was his birthright, after all, even if his old man would be mad as well when he found out.

But those were the breaks, weren't they? His father Deke's attitude was one of the things that had driven Christopher to Red Rock in the first place. Once he was settled, he'd gone to court and filed a petition to change his name. Once the judge had signed the order, Christopher Fortune said *Hasta la vista, baby* to Chris Jones and Horseback Hollow and claimed what was rightfully his.

Christopher glanced around his office, trying to see it through Toby's eyes. The Fortune Foundation had been founded in memory of Lily Cassidy Fortune's late husband, Ryan Fortune, who had died of a brain tumor nine years ago. The Foundation had started out in a small storefront on Main Street in downtown Red Rock but had since expanded and was now located in a stately three-story brick building just outside of town. Christopher had one of the corner offices with rich polished mahogany architectural wall paneling on the walls—or at least the ones that didn't have floor-to-ceiling windows with a to-die-for view of the local landscape. His traditional executive's desk and credenza still left enough room for the putting green, two chairs and a couch that were grouped conversation-style around a coffee table.

Well, his office was bigger than his old studio apartment back in Horseback Hollow.

He directed Toby and Angie over to the couch. Until now, he hadn't even tried out the office's living room furniture.

"I just can't get over the change in you," Toby said.

Christopher turned to Angie, who was still as pretty as she had been in high school with her light brown hair, blue eyes and delicate features. His brother had done well catching her. He'd tell him so later if they had a private moment. But just as the thought crossed his mind, it was overshadowed by the hope that the newlyweds weren't planning an extended visit in Red Rock. Christopher had work to do.

He hoped this visit wasn't because Deke had sent Toby to do his dirty work. If any of his family got him it was Toby. But it would be just like Deke to send one of Christopher's brothers to hassle him.

But right now, Toby was talking to Angie. "The Chris I knew never wore anything but jeans and boots. I don't know who this suit is standing in front of me with those shiny pointy-toed shoes. How many crocodiles had to die to make those shoes?"

Christopher laughed, but it was a dry, humorless sound. "They're not made out of crocodile," Christopher said.

"It was a joke, Chris." Toby frowned. "No offense, but you're even acting differently. Just remember, I know where you came from."

Awkward silence the likes of which he had never known with Toby hung in the air. He didn't want to fight with him, and it seemed every time he opened his mouth he said the wrong thing.

That was the story of his life when it came to family. But Christopher wasn't about to sit here in his own office and let family drag him down to feeling bad.

"How was the wedding?" Christopher asked, hoping for neutral ground. He directed the question to Angie, who had been remarkably quiet.

"I would say it was the happiest day of my

life, but each day I wake up seems to take that title," she said. "We wish you could've been there."

"Yeah, well, it's better that I didn't come. That way the focus was on the two of you. All sunshine and happiness. No dark clouds, you know?"

Angie looked at him with big blue eyes.

"Well, we certainly did appreciate your generous gift. A thousand dollars was…" Angie shook her head as if at a loss for words.

"It was too much," said Toby as he leaned forward and plucked a business card out of a brass holder sitting on the coffee table. "Ten crisp $100 bills. Leave it to my little brother not to miss an opportunity to show off— Wait. Christopher *Fortune?*" he read aloud from the business card. "Did they forget to print your entire last name on here?"

"No," said Christopher.

Toby held up the card. "Where's the *Jones?*"

Christopher shrugged, but didn't feel the need to explain himself.

"So, that's why the receptionist was having a hard time helping us." Toby gestured with his thumb toward the reception area. "It's true, then? They don't even know who Chris Jones is?"

"Don't take it personally, Toby," Christopher said. "I just needed to make a fresh start."

"How can I not take it personally? I mean, I get that you and Dad don't see eye to eye on your moving to Red Rock and working here at the Foundation, but come on, Chris. What the hell? Aren't you taking this a little too far?"

"Is that a question or an accusation?" Christopher challenged, holding his brother's gaze until Toby leaned forward again and put the card back where he'd found it.

This life was exactly what he wanted.

He wanted what the Fortunes had: money, power, respect. He had gotten none of that back in Horseback Hollow. What was wrong with claiming it now?

"I figure the family can't be any more disappointed in me now than they've always been. I never was any good to anyone around the ranch, anyway. Don't you think they'd consider the new and improved Christopher Fortune a vast improvement over Chris Jones, the son who couldn't do anything right?"

Toby looked down at his hands, then back up at Christopher. A somber expression crept into his eyes. "I don't even know what to say to that, except that Mom asked me to tell you she loves you."

*Touché.*

That was just about the only thing that Toby could've said to hit Christopher where he'd feel it.

The thing was, he didn't even sound mad. Just…disappointed. A look that said, *remember where you came from and don't let the Fortunes change you into something you're not.*

He hadn't forgotten and the Fortunes hadn't changed him. He would be the first to admit that embracing the Fortunes' world and starting on a desk job had taken some getting used to. He was surprised by how he sometimes missed not getting outside between the hours of nine and five. This indoor, sedentary job had been a challenge, but every time he looked at the view outside the windows of his executive's office or at his bank account balance, it got easier and easier.

"Y'all must be hungry," Christopher said. "Come on, let's go get a bite to eat. I'll treat you to lunch."

"Excuse me, darlin'." Kinsley Aaron frowned as she looked up from the notes she was taking while manning the third-floor reception desk for Bev. Christopher Fortune stood outside his office door, smiling broadly, no doubt thinking he was God's gift to women.

*Darlin'? Excuse me?*

Had they somehow time traveled back to the 1960s?

"My name is Kinsley," she said, doing her best to keep the bristle out of her voice. He may have been young and good-looking and a Fortune, but how dare he call her that?

"I know what your name is," Christopher said.

"Then why did you call me *darlin'*?" She didn't smile.

The man and woman who were with him looked a bit sheepish, perhaps a little embarrassed for him, before they ducked back inside his office. Actually, Christopher should've been embarrassed for himself. But did the guy do anything for himself?

The only reason he worked at the Foundation was because his uncle was James Marshall Fortune.

"Where is Betsy?" he asked

"Who is Betsy?" she returned.

"The new receptionist?" he answered with a tone better suited for talking to a small child.

*Well, Mr. Man, two could play that game.*

"Nobody by the name of *Betsy* works here. Do you mean *Beverly?*"

Christopher shrugged. "Yes, the one who was here earlier." He motioned to the desk where Kinsley was sitting. "Where is she?"

*If Bev was smart, she'd handed in her resignation and left.*

Kinsley blinked away the snotty thought. She hadn't meant it. The Fortune Foundation was a fabulous place to work. Even though Christopher Fortune was full of himself, other members of the Fortune family had been very good to her. Not only did they pay her a decent salary to work as an outreach coordinator, a position she considered her life's work, but also she would be forever grateful that they had taken a chance on her.

She'd come to them with little experience, having not yet earned her degree. She was working on it, but with a full-time job and going to school part-time at night, it was going to take her a while before she completed her coursework.

"I'm covering for Beverly while she's on her break," Kinsley said. "She should be back in about fifteen minutes. In the meantime, is there something I can help you with?"

Christopher smiled and looked at her in

that wolfish way he had that made her want to squirm. But she didn't. No way. She wouldn't give him the satisfaction.

What was with this guy? Better question, what was with her? Kinsley had always sub-scribed to the Eleanor Roosevelt philosophy: nobody could make you feel *anything* unless you gave them permission. Actually, the quote was nobody could make you feel inferior, but this adaptation felt just as authentic.

"Yes, will you please call and make a lunch reservation for three at Red for 1:15?"

At first Kinsley thought he was kidding. But as she squinted at him, it became quite clear that he was indeed serious.

News flash! She had not been hired as Chris-topher Fortune's personal secretary! And why did he want to eat at Red, of all places, today? She rarely went out to lunch, but today she had a 12:45 business lunch at the restaurant. She was meeting Meg Tyler, the Red Rock High School PTA president, to discuss the school's Cornerstone Club, an extracurricular student leadership organization, and to talk about the role the kids could play in implementing an anti-bullying program.

For a split second, Kinsley thought about calling Meg and asking if they could change restaurants, but then quickly decided against it. She'd been looking forward to lunch at Red. Why should she deny herself her favorite Mexican place just because he was going to be there?

Yeah, what was up with that? Why was she still feeling so shy around him? He'd started working with the Foundation about two months ago. They hadn't had much contact until recently, when Emmett Jamison had asked them to work together to establish a stronger online presence for the Foundation's community outreach program.

Why did she allow him to make her feel twelve years old? Worse yet, why did she shrink every time Christopher walked into the room? She didn't need his approval. So what if he was charismatic and good-looking? He skated through life on his looks and charm, much like her father had done when he was sober. At least she did her job better than he did.

Fighting the riptide of emotions that threatened to sweep her under, Kinsley stared unseeing at the notes she'd been writing before Christopher had come out of his office. She wasn't going to allow herself to be drowned by the past. Her father had been dead for six years, and she certainly wasn't twelve anymore. In all fairness, despite Christopher's bravado, he really didn't have the mean streak that had possessed her father when he had been drunk. That was when her dad had drummed it into her soul that she would never amount to anything. That she wouldn't be good enough, strong enough, smart enough, pretty enough. No man in his right mind would ever want her.

But that was then and this was now. She was well on her way to proving him wrong. She had a good job, and she was making her own way in the world. No matter how the scarred memories of her bastard of a father tried to convince her that she would never be enough, she needed to muster the strength to exorcise his ghost and set herself free. She needed to quit projecting her father and his twisted ways onto Christopher, who, like so many other men, had a way of making her feel overlooked, dismissed.

She knew her value and what she was capable of. That was all that mattered.

Because she was sitting at the reception desk filling in for Bev, she swallowed her pride and placed the call to Red. A few minutes later, Christopher and his posse emerged from his office and made their way to the elevator. But

Christopher hung back. "Thanks for taking care of my family and me, Kinsley."

He looked her square in the eyes in that brazen way of his and flashed a smile. For a short, stupid moment part of her went soft and breathless.

"Mmm" was all she managed to say before she tore her gaze from his and he walked away to join his party.

*Mmm.* Not even a real word. Just an embarrassing monosyllabic grunt.

Kinsley sat at the reception desk waiting for Bev to return, pondering the shyness that always seemed to get the better of her whenever he was around.

*Why?*

Why did he have this effect on her?

It was because this job meant so much to her.

And maybe she found his good looks a little intimidating. But good grief.

So the guy was attractive with his perfectly chiseled features and those mile-wide broad shoulders. He had probably played football in college. One of those cocky jock types who had a harem clamoring to serve him. Not that Christopher Fortune's personal life—past or present—was any of her business.

Kinsley blinked and mentally backed away

from thoughts of her coworker. Instead, she reminded herself that she had done the right thing by taking the high road and making his darned lunch reservation rather than trying to make a point.

Looks didn't matter. Not in her world, anyway. She had Christopher Fortune's number. He was a handsome opportunist who was riding his family's coattails. In the two months he'd been in the office he hadn't done much to prove that he had high regard for the actual work they were trying to do at the Foundation.

Obviously, he didn't *get it*. Guys like him never did.

But one thing she was going to make sure he understood in no uncertain terms—he'd better never call her *darlin'* again or there would be hell to pay.

## Chapter 2

"Oh, look at the flowers." Angie sighed as Christopher guided her and Toby up the bougainvillea-lined path to Red.

"Just wait until you see the courtyard inside," Christopher said with as much pride as if he were showing off his own home. "Red is built around it. There's a fountain I think you'll love."

Angie stopped. "Red?"

"Yes, that's the name of the restaurant." Christopher gestured to the tile nameplate attached to the wall just outside the door, which he held open as he tried to usher them inside, but Angie stopped.

"Is this the same Red that's owned by the Mendozas?" Angie asked.

"One and the same," Christopher said.

"Wendy and Marcos Mendoza catered our wedding reception." Angie sighed again as she looked around, taking it all in. "They have to be two of the nicest people I've ever met." She turned to Toby. "I can't believe we're here. Chris, did you plan this?"

He wished he could take credit for it, but until now, he'd had no idea what had taken place at their wedding. He'd been so intent on staying away to avoid clouding their day with bad vibes that he hadn't realized he didn't know the first thing about the event other than the fact that his brother had taken himself a bride.

Regret knotted in his gut.

"The Mendozas catered your wedding?" Christopher asked.

"Yes, they did a beautiful job," Angie said. "Everything was delicious. Oh, I hope that chicken mole they served at the reception is on the menu. I've been dreaming of it ever since."

A twinge of disappointment wove itself around the regret. Christopher knew it was totally irrational, but he had brought them here because he'd wanted to introduce them

to something new, something from his world
that he had discovered. Yet by a strange twist
of small-world fate, Red was old news to them.

"This place is so beautiful," Angie cooed.
"I could live here quite comfortably."

"I'll bet we could." Toby beamed at his wife.
His love for her was written all over his face.
Watching the two of them so deeply in love
blunted the edges of Christopher's disappointment. He wasn't surprised that Toby had settled down. Of all of his siblings, Toby had been
the one who was the most family oriented, especially after taking in the three Hemings kids.
He was happy for his brother and Angie. He
hoped things worked out and that they would
be able to adopt the kids. But although Christopher looked forward to being an uncle, he
couldn't imagine any other kind of life than
the one he was living now.

On their way to lunch Christopher had
seized the opportunity to show off his new
town and lifestyle. He'd loaded the newlyweds
into his spankin' new BMW and given them
the fifty cent tour of downtown Red Rock.

Although there were certainly fancier restaurants in town, none spoke to Christopher
quite the way Red did. Obviously the Mendoza
appeal wasn't restricted to Red Rock, since

Toby and Angie seemed to love their food as much as he did.

Christopher held open the door as Angie and Toby stepped inside. He breathed in deeply as he followed them. It smelled damn good...of fresh corn tortillas, chilies and spices. There was something about the mix of old and new that appealed to him. The restaurant was housed in a converted hacienda that had once been owned by a Spanish family rumored to have been related to Mexican dignitary Antonio López de Santa Ana. Santa Ana was known as the Napoleon of the West. Christopher had recently learned that the current owners of the property, Jose and Maria Mendoza, had been fortunate to purchase the house and land at an affordable price before anyone realized its historical significance. The place couldn't have been in better hands because the Mendozas had given the place its due reverence. That was especially true after the restaurant had been largely destroyed by an arson fire in 2009. Luckily, the family rebuilt and reopened after several months and had been going strong ever since.

Inside, the restaurant was decorated with antiques, paintings and memorabilia that dated all the way back to 1845 when President James

Polk named Texas the twenty-eighth state of the Union.

In college, Christopher had complemented his business major with a history minor. So it was only natural that he liked the place for its history.

But the food...he *loved* the place for its food.

Red offered a mouthwatering selection of nouveau Mexican cuisine. The chef had a talent for taking traditional dishes such as huevos rancheros, the chicken mole that Angie was so crazy about and tamales, and sending them to new heights using fresh twists on old classics. The menu was bright and vibrant, familiar yet new and exciting.

Christopher had experienced nothing like it in Horseback Hollow. His mother, Jeanne Marie, was a great cook, but her repertoire was more of the meat and potatoes/comfort food variety. The food at Red was an exotic and surprising twist on traditional Mexican.

The chef was always coming up with new specials of the day and anytime Christopher was in, he asked him to taste test and share his opinion. Christopher loved being able to offer his input.

"Good afternoon, Mr. Fortune," said the hostess. "We're so glad you chose to join us for lunch today. Come right this way. Your favorite table is ready."

The shapely brunette shot Christopher a sexy smile before she turned, hips swaying, as she led the three of them to an aged pine table next to a large window where they could enjoy the comfort of the air-conditioning, but still look out at the well-landscaped courtyard. As far as Christopher was concerned, it was the best seat in the house.

After they were settled, the hostess handed each of them a menu. "Enjoy your lunch, and please let me know if you need *anything*."

She winked at Christopher before she turned to make her way back to the hostess station.

That was quite obvious of her, Christopher thought as he watched her walk away on her high-high heels with the grace and assurance of a tightrope walker. Her skirt was just short enough to draw the eye down to her firm, tanned calves. Now, that was a woman who knew how to dress. Unlike Kinsley, who hid herself under all that heavy tweed fabric that left her looking buttoned-up and shapeless. What a shame.

Suddenly, seeing Kinsley in a skirt and heels like that became his new fantasy.

"I see you come here for the good service," Toby said, a knowing glint in his eye.

"Of course." As Christopher turned back to his brother and Angie, a blonde caught his eye. She was was seated at a table to their left—and he couldn't help noticing that she resembled Kinsley—

*Wait, that* is *Kinsley.*

She was dining with a woman he didn't recognize. He had a view of Kinsley's profile. If she just turned her head ever so slightly to the right she would see him, but she seemed engrossed in her conversation. Just as he was contemplating getting up and going over to say hello, her server brought their food.

She must have gotten here before him and ordered already. Besides, he, Toby and Angie had just sat down. They hadn't even placed their drink order. He would wait.

When she'd made his reservation she hadn't mentioned that she'd be dining here herself, even though she knew he was going to be here right around the same time. Maybe she was afraid that he would think she was angling for an invite to join them. Most of the women he knew wouldn't have been shy about doing that. But Kinsley was different. Quiet, understated, more conservative.

She was a refreshing change from all the other women he'd met since he'd been in Red Rock. And there had been more than a few. Most of them were sassy and assertive, not at all afraid to reach out and let him know exactly what they wanted and how they wanted it. None of them was a keeper, either. They were all nice and fun, of course, but they left him wanting.

Kinsley, on the other hand, was a puzzle, and most definitely, he realized as he was sitting there, one he was interested in trying to solve.

Hmm. Why had he never thought about her like that before? He'd always thought she was pretty, and on occasion he'd tried to flirt with her, but until right now, he'd never really thought about what made her tick.

As if she felt him watching her, she glanced his way, and their gazes snared. He waved and she lifted a finger before turning her attention back to her lunch companion.

Despite this strange new Kinsley-awareness coursing through him, Christopher decided he should do the same and turned his focus to his brother and Angie. But pushing her from his mind was harder than he had expected.

The view of the courtyard helped. It was

spectacular, with colorful Talavera tiles scattered here and there on the stucco walls, Mexican fan trees and more thriving bougainvillea that seemed to be blooming overtime today in a riot of hot pink, purple and gold. But even the crowning glory of the stately, large fountain in the center of the courtyard couldn't keep Christopher's gaze from wandering over Kinsley's way.

"Too bad we couldn't sit outside," Toby said.

If the temperature wasn't pushing ninety, Christopher would've insisted that they sit out by the fountain. Even though the outside tables were shaded by colorful umbrellas, the humidity was a killer. He didn't want to sweat through his suit and then go back to work.

Not the image he wanted to portray, he thought, glancing at Kinsley.

"Is this okay?" he asked Toby and Angie. "We could move, but it's a killer out there."

"No, this is so lovely," said Angie. "I want to stay right here."

Before she could say more, Marcos Mendoza, the manager of Red, appeared at their table.

"Christopher Fortune, my man." Marcos and Christopher shook hands. "It's great to see you."

"You, too," said Christopher. "My brother Toby and his wife, Angie, are visiting. I couldn't let them leave Red Rock without dining at Red."

"Well, if it isn't the newlyweds." Marcos leaned in and kissed Angie on the cheek then shook Toby's hand. He hooked a thumb in Christopher's direction. "This guy is your brother?"

"Yep, I'll claim him," Toby said without a second's hesitation. His brother's conviction caused Christopher's heart to squeeze ever so slightly, but he did a mental two-step away from the emotion and everything else it implied: the problems between him and Deke; the way he'd left home; the fact that he'd allowed all the ugliness to cause him to miss his own brother's wedding.

"Christopher here is one of our best customers," Marcos said. "I can't believe I didn't put two and two together and figure out that the two of you were related. But different last names?"

"I go by Fortune. Toby goes by Fortune Jones." Angie flinched. Christopher hadn't meant to bite out the words. There was a beat of awkward silence before Toby changed the subject.

"Did you know that Marcos and Wendy are opening a new restaurant in Horseback Hollow?" he asked Christopher.

"Seriously?" Christopher said. He'd only been away a couple of months and he felt like a stranger.

"We're opening The Hollows Cantina next month. In fact, my wife, Wendy, and I are in the process of packing up and moving there with our daughter, MaryAnne." Marcos paused, a thoughtful look washing over his face. He turned to Christopher. "So if you and Toby are brothers, that means Liam Fortune Jones is your brother, too?"

Christopher nodded.

Marcos smiled. "I've hired his fiancée, Julia Tierney, to be the assistant manager at the restaurant."

Christopher forced a smile.

"I had no idea that you were leaving Red Rock, or that Julia would be working for you," Christopher said.

"I kept it on the down low until I was sure that everything would pan out," said Marcos. "This is a great opportunity for my family, and having my own restaurant will be a dream come true. Really, we owe this happy decision to Julia. She is the one who talked us into opening a place in Horseback Hollow. Your future sister-in-law should work for the Horseback Hollow Chamber of Commerce— she can't say enough good about the place."

"Congratulations," said Angie. "We will be sure to come in after the Cantina opens."

"I have your contact information," said Marcos, "and I will make sure that the two of you are invited to the grand opening. The Fortunes are like family, and family always sticks together."

Toby shot Christopher a knowing look. "Yes, they do."

"In fact, Fortune," Marcos said to Christopher, "I'd better see you at the grand opening celebration, too. Especially now that I know that you're a native son of Horseback Hollow."

Christopher gave a wry smile. "Yeah, well, don't go spreading that around."

Everybody laughed, unaware or ignoring the fact that Christopher wasn't kidding.

"I need to get back to work," Marcos said. "So please excuse me and enjoy your lunch."

The men shook hands again and Marcos planted another kiss on Angie's cheek before he moved on to greet the next table of guests.

"When are Julia and Liam getting married?" asked Christopher.

"That remains to be seen," said Toby. "It's a big step that he's committed to one woman. Julia is good for him. She gets him, but doesn't let him get away with squat. I think she's about the only woman who could make an honest man out of him."

Nodding, Christopher gave the menu a cursory glance. He wanted to hear the day's specials, but it would take something extra appealing to sway him away from his favorite beef brisket enchiladas.

Toby looked up from his menu. "It looks like the marriage bug is infesting our family. I just heard that our cousin Amelia Chesterfield Fortune has gotten engaged to some British aristocrat."

"That just seems so odd," mused Angie. "She was dancing with Quinn Drummond at our wedding. It was the way they were looking at each other... The two of them seemed so happy. In fact, I would've wagered that something was blossoming between them. I just can't imagine that there's another man in the picture."

"Yeah, but I heard the news from Mama and she usually gets things right." Toby shook his head as if trying to reconcile the idea.

Their server was a woman named DeeDee.

Christopher had seen her socially one time, but he hadn't called her again. He hadn't realized that she worked at Red. Within the first hour of their date, he'd realized DeeDee was after a whole lot more relationship than he was able to give. No sense in stringing her along, even if she was nice. The world was full of nice women and he needed to get to know a lot more of them before he settled down. He found his gaze sliding over to Kinsley's table yet again. It looked as if they were finishing up with their meals. "Well, if it isn't Christopher Fortune as I live and breathe," DeeDee said, a teasing note in her voice. She twisted a strand of her long red hair around her finger as she talked. "It's been so long since I heard from you, I thought maybe you'd fallen off the face of the earth or maybe you moved to some exotic, faraway land."

Christopher laughed, keeping things light. "It's good to see you, DeeDee. How long have you been working here?"

"It's only my second day."

"Which explains why I've never seen you here," said Christopher.

After a little more playful banter, DeeDee flipped her hair off her shoulder with a swift swipe of her hand and took their drink orders.

Next, she described the day's specials, which didn't tempt Christopher's taste buds away from his usual order. After she left to get their drinks, Christopher recommended some of his favorites from the menu to Toby and Angie.

A few minutes later DeeDee returned with a bottle of champagne and three flutes. "This is for the newlyweds, compliments of Mr. Mendoza and the staff at Red."

"Oh, my goodness," said Angie. "Champagne in the middle of the day. How decadent. And how absolutely lovely. Thank you."

"Well, the way I see it," said Toby, "I'm only getting married once, and it's an occasion to celebrate. Right, little brother?"

Toby didn't wait for Christopher to answer. He put his arm around his bride and leaned in, placing a sound kiss on Angie's lips. If DeeDee hadn't been standing there, Christopher might have joked and told them to get a room. But really, it was nice to see Toby and Angie so happy.

"So this is your brother and sister-in-law?" asked DeeDee after she popped the cork and filled the glasses with the bubbly.

Christopher didn't want to be rude, but he didn't want to get too personal. "Yes," he said.

"They're visiting, but I'm on my lunch hour so we should place our orders now."

"Of course," said DeeDee, snapping into professional mode. She wrote down their selections and headed toward the kitchen.

After she left, Christopher said, "I just can't get over the fact that you're *married*. But it suits you. It really does."

Toby gave Angie a little squeeze.

"Where do the adoption proceedings stand?" Christopher asked. Seven months ago, Toby had taken in the Hemings children: eleven-year-old Brian, eight-year-old Justin and seven-year-old Kylie. The kids had had nowhere to turn and faced possible separation when their aunt was ordered into rehab for a drinking problem and child neglect. Both Christopher and Toby had known the kids from the Vicker's Corners YMCA where they had worked as coaches. Most people would've run from that kind of responsibility—Christopher knew he certainly couldn't have handled it—but Toby hadn't thought twice before agreeing to take them in.

Unfortunately, the kids' aunt, who obviously didn't have the children's best interests at heart, had decided to try and take the kids from Toby and send them into another unstable situation in California. Her reasoning was the kids should be with relatives. Never mind that the relative she'd chosen was out of work and on parole.

That's all it took for Toby to decide he needed to legally adopt the children.

"Everything is still pending," said Toby. "Frankly, it's taking so long I'm starting to get worried."

"I just don't understand what the holdup is," said Angie. "They not only have a loving home with us, but they also have become part of the family. They call Jeanne Marie and Deke Grandma and Grandpa. They're calling your sisters and brothers Aunt and Uncle. How anyone could think that uprooting these poor kids is what's best for them is beyond me. It breaks my heart."

Toby caressed Angie's shoulder. "We are going to do everything in our power to make sure they stay with us."

"What can I do to help?" asked Christopher.

Toby shrugged. "At this point I don't know what else anyone could do."

"The Fortune name carries a lot of clout," said Christopher. "Maybe we can use its influence to get things going in the right direction."

Toby peered at him. "What exactly are you suggesting?"

Christopher gave a one-shoulder shrug as he rubbed the fingers of his left hand together in the international gesture for *money*. "Money talks, bro."

Toby frowned and shook his head. "Please don't even suggest anything like that. I don't want to be accused of doing anything unethical. That might hurt the situation more than it helps."

"Nonsense," said Christopher. "I think you're being very shortsighted if you don't take full advantage of your birthright."

Christopher saw Toby take in a slow deep breath, as he always did when faced with conflict. It was as if he were framing his response so that he didn't lose his cool.

"I appreciate your concern, Chris," said Toby evenly. "But the caseworker told me she's worried that the Fortunes themselves may be part of the problem. Since the Fortunes invaded Horseback Hollow so many strange things have happened. The authorities still think Orlando Mendoza's accident might have been directed at the family."

"Don't be ridiculous," said Christopher. "Why would anyone want to hurt the Fortunes? I mean, look at me. I'm living proof. Since I changed my name nothing bad has happened to me."

Christopher turned his palms up to punctuate his point.

"That is, if you don't count your running away from home and shunning your entire family as something bad."

Toby cocked an eyebrow at Christopher.

Christopher locked gazes with his brother and crossed his arms.

"Look, I know this Fortune Foundation gig is still new and exciting to you," said Toby, "so don't take this wrong. But someday you're going to learn that some things are more important than money."

Christopher glanced over at Kinsley, but she and her friend were gone. His gaze swept the restaurant, but she was nowhere to be seen. How had he not seen her leave?

He picked up his champagne glass and knocked back the contents.

"Come on, Chris," said Toby. "When are you coming home? No one has seen you in months. They certainly have no idea that you've completely disowned Daddy's name."

Toby was usually the only one who could see Christopher's side in times when he and

Deke disagreed, which was more often than not. Awkward silence hung in the air and, for once, Christopher didn't know how to fill it. He didn't want to fight with Toby, but he wasn't going back to Horseback Hollow. His life was here now, and he would prefer to keep his old and new lives separate. The contrast between the Joneses and the Fortunes was stark. Christopher couldn't take the chance of losing the respect he'd earned at the Foundation.

"Man up, Chris," Toby urged. "Take the high road and be the one who extends the olive branch to Deke."

"Yeah, well that high road has two lanes. Deke can bring that olive branch to me easier than I can bring it to him. I'm a little too busy right now to coddle a grown man."

Toby made a *tsk* sound. "An *old* man. Don't wait too long. You may be sorry if you do."

"Don't pull that guilt trip crap on me," said Christopher. "Just don't. But please do tell me why it's okay for Deke to resent me for making an honest living in a career I love. For making my own way. For not having dirt under my fingernails. No offense to you, but why should I have to grovel to him because the ranch life is not the kind of life I want? Until Deke understands that, I don't think we're going to meet anywhere, much less with an olive branch."

Truth be told, he would rather be known as James Marshall Fortune's nephew than as the son of Deke Jones, crusty old cattle rancher. Christopher hoped that Toby wouldn't make him come out and say that.

Toby stared at Christopher, looking thin-lipped and angry.

"So you've got the fancy suits, the brand-new car and a parade of women who think you're a big shot," said Toby, virtually rolling his eyes at what he obviously perceived as self-importance. "Looks like you've finally achieved your dream, haven't you?"

"You shouldn't knock it since you've never tried it," said Christopher. "No offense to you, Angie. I'm just saying."

Toby took his wife's hand and laced his fingers through hers. "No loss. Believe me, I wouldn't trade my life for yours. I couldn't possibly be any happier than I am with Angie and the kids. On that note, I think we'd better start heading toward home."

Toby pulled out his wallet and tossed a crisp $100 bill onto the table in payment for the food they hadn't managed to stay long enough to have delivered to their table. It was probably one of the ten that Christopher had given him as a wedding gift.

Christopher slid the bill back toward his brother. "Here, Toby. I've got this."

Toby stood. "No, you don't. If you *got this,* you would stop acting like such a pretentious jackass and come home and make amends with Dad. You may have given up on us, Chris, but we'll never give up on you. Take care of yourself and call me when you're ready to talk."

## Chapter 3

With his long lunches and daily putting practice, was it any wonder Christopher Fortune didn't get much done? Kinsley mused after fielding a call from Emmett Jamison, the head of the Foundation. Even so, she'd covered for Christopher when Mr. Jamison had asked if she'd seen him. She'd explained that he'd taken a late lunch with family visiting from out of town. She didn't mention that he'd been gone nearly two-and-a-half hours.

She may not have agreed with the way Christopher conducted himself, but she wasn't about to throw him under the bus. That would just make her look bad in the eyes of Mr. Jamison.

She wanted him to see her as a problem solver, not the type of person who pointed fingers and ratted people out. Besides, with the Fortunes, blood was definitely thicker than water. If she wasn't careful the situation might get turned around and come back to bite her. She was sure if it came down to her or Christopher Fortune, Emmett Jamison would side with the man whose last name was on his paycheck.

Kinsley drummed her fingers on the desk. The Fortunes were all about family. She knew Mr. Jamison would excuse him for that. She couldn't deny that she envied Christopher and his huge support system. What was it like to come from such a large, protective family that would circle the wagons at a moment's notice?

Kinsley had no idea. Growing up the only child of an alcoholic father and a mother who couldn't stand up for herself didn't give her much experience to draw from.

She and her mother only had each other to intervene when her father was on a drunken bender. When they did stand up to him, there was always hell to pay.

Her grandmother—her mom's mom—had passed away when Kinsley was about eight, but Grandma hadn't had the wherewithal to extract her daughter from what Kinsley would later look back on and realize was a situation that had robbed her mother of her life.

But wasn't hindsight always perfect?

From the moment Kinsley was old enough to realize she could take care of herself, she vowed she would never personally depend on a man. For that matter, she preferred to not depend on anyone, because didn't people always let you down?

She'd only had two boyfriends, and both of them had proven that to be true. They were hard lessons, but she'd learned. And she prided herself on not repeating the same mistakes.

Family ranks or not, Emmett had said he was concerned because he had received a call from a woman named Judy Davis who was perplexed because she'd emailed the community relations office three times about a donation she wanted to make and still hadn't heard back. She was beginning to think the Foundation didn't want her money.

Kinsley made an excuse that there had been technical difficulties with the email account and had assured Mr. Jamison that she and Christopher would make sure everything was working as it should as soon as he got back... which should be any minute.

*Technically,* Christopher was being *difficult.*

Right? Did that count as technical difficulties? She hoped so. Because it was all she had.

She would cover for Christopher this time, but they were definitely going to have a little heart to heart.

She wrote down Judy Davis's information and assured Mr. Jamison that they would follow up with her today and make sure she knew how much her donation was needed and appreciated.

Kinsley's cheeks burned.

She didn't appreciate being left holding the bag for matters like this, especially when it was something Christopher had insisted on handling. The new Foundation Community Relations email address had been her idea, but they had decided to split the work: as she went out into the community, Kinsley would get the word out about the new way to contact the Foundation; as vice president of community relations, Christopher had insisted on being the one to respond to the emails.

Thank goodness Kinsley had insisted on knowing the password. Christopher had agreed that it was a good idea for more than one person to have access to the account, but he had assured her that he would check it regularly. She had taken him at his word. Kinsley mentally kicked herself for trusting so blindly. People might have been reaching out for help or there could be more potential funding for the Foundation in these unread messages. Yet Christopher was too busy perfecting his putt… and she'd covered for him.

Feeling like a fool, Kinsley gritted her teeth as she typed in the URL to bring up the login page so she could sign into the account.

As a Fortune, Christopher was set for life. Unlike the other family members who worked at the Foundation, he didn't seem grounded in the realities of what mere mortals had to face in the world.

No, Christopher Fortune was fat, spoiled and smug—

Well, maybe not fat. Kinsley hated herself for it, but somehow her gaze always managed to find its way to Christopher's abs. The way his expensive, tailored dress shirts tapered in at his trim waist, she could plainly see that the guy didn't have an ounce of fat on his body.

No, he was all broad shoulders and six-pack abs—or at least she imagined he was sporting a six-pack under his buttoned up exterior. Who wouldn't be if they had time to work out daily? Actually, it didn't matter what Christopher Fortune was packing under his crisp cotton shirt. Mr. Vice President was still spoiled and smug. And completely irresponsible when it came to doing his job.

When the login page came up, she was relieved to see that it hadn't been that long since Christopher had checked the account. In fact, it had only been two days. She scrolled through the ten emails in search of Judy Davis's three messages. When she found them, she realized the three emails had arrived within a span of 36 hours.

Mr. Jamison had been under the impression that she'd been waiting a long time to hear back. Though it really hadn't been an excessively long time since Christopher had checked the account, it did need to be monitored regularly. Several times a day, in fact, to keep something like this from happening.

If that was too much for Christopher to handle, he needed to hand it over to someone who could keep a closer eye on it, Kinsley thought as she started to click on one of the unopened message.

But then she stopped. Instead, she had a better idea.

She took a screenshot of the emails that still needed attention and printed it out. Then she took a fluorescent yellow highlighter and marked each one that he needed to check.

She'd already covered for him. If she did his work for him, too, she would simply be fostering his habit of letting someone else pick up the pieces.

The thought took her back to another place and time that made her unspeakably sad. Maybe if she'd intervened a little more on behalf of her mother things would've turned out differently. She stared at the computer screen as the memory threatened to cut into her heart. But she shrugged off the feelings before they could take root. What had happened to her mother was entirely different from what was happening now. No amount of wishing or dwelling would change the way things had played out. That's why Kinsley's job at the Foundation was so important. She couldn't change the past, but maybe, if she did her job well, she could make a difference for someone else.

Christopher Fortune didn't need saving. He needed a good swift kick in the rear.

Kinsley had her own workload to worry about. The last thing she needed was to try and reform Mr. Silver Spoon. He was a big boy; he could take care of himself. He needed to start pulling his load. She fully intended to tell him as much when he got back.

Well…in so many words.

She wasn't going to do anything to jeopardize her job. But she could still stand up for herself.

This would be a good time to make sure Christopher knew that, although she didn't mind helping him out with things like checking the Foundation's Community Relations email account and making his lunch reservations, she wasn't his secretary. She didn't intend to mince words about that.

She paper clipped Judy Davis's contact information on top of the highlighted list of unanswered emails and set the papers on the corner of her desk.

She knew it wasn't her place to call him out; she intended to do it tactfully. She'd make him think it was all his idea. But yes. They were going to have a little reality check when he got back. She glanced at the clock on her cell phone—was he even coming back to the office today?

She picked up the phone and dialed. "Hi, Bev, would you please let me know when Mr. Fortune gets back into the office? I want to schedule a meeting with him."

"Speak of the devil," Bev whispered. "He just walked in from lunch. Want me to see if he's available?"

"No, that's okay," Kinsley said. "I'll just walk down the hall and stick my head in his office."

Christopher swiveled his office chair so that it faced the window. He leaned back, stretching his legs out in front of him and resting his hands on his middle.

The more he thought about what had happened at lunch, the more he was sure Deke had sent Toby to do his bidding. It made him so angry he wanted to wrap his putter around the trunk of the magnolia tree out in front of the building.

It could've been a good visit with his brother. A chance to get to know his new sister-in-law a little better. But Deke had to insert himself, even if it was virtually, and mess things up.

His father was so good at messing things up.

But then Christopher had to wonder if his brother would've come to Red Rock if it hadn't been to prod him to go home. Well, it hadn't done any good. If anything it had given him more incentive to stay away. The Joneses couldn't stand anything that varied from their idea of normal. But Christopher had news for them all—this was his new normal.

He looked up at the sound of a knock on his door. He straightened up in his chair and turned back to his desk, moving the mouse to wake up his computer screen.

"Come in," he said.

He was delighted when he saw Kinsley standing in the threshold. Suddenly the afternoon was looking a lot brighter.

"Do you have a moment?" she asked.

"For you, I would clear my schedule."

She rolled her eyes. Not exactly the response he was hoping for, but he would've been surprised if he'd gotten a more enthused reaction.

"I'm just kidding," he said. Actually, he wasn't. "Come in. I'm not the big bad wolf. How was your lunch?"

She shut the door and walked over to stand in front of his desk. "It was fine."

"I saw you at Red," he said. "I was going to come over and say hello, but by the time we ordered you were gone."

"I only had an hour for lunch. I had to get back."

Since he'd seen her at the restaurant she'd pulled her hair back away from her face. And what a face it was; she had a perfect complexion that didn't require much makeup. In fact, he wasn't even sure if she was wearing any makeup. His mind wandered for a moment, imagining the curves that hid beneath the conservative clothes she wore. He smiled at the thought. But then he realized she wasn't smiling at him.

God, if he didn't know better, he might be afraid she'd read his mind.

"Is something wrong?" he asked.

"Since you asked," she said, "actually, yes, there is something wrong."

She held out a piece of paper. He reached across the desk and took it from her.

"What's this?"

She was standing there with her arms crossed—defensive body language. Her sensible blue blouse was buttoned all the way up to the top and was tucked into a plain lighter blue skirt that didn't show nearly enough leg. Legs, he thought, that would look killer in a pair of shiny black stilettos, ones like the hostess at Red had worn, rather than those low-heeled church lady shoes that looked like something out of his mama's closet.

"It's a message from a woman who has been trying to get a hold of you to make a donation to the Foundation," she said.

Christopher read the name and number scrawled on the paper. Judy Davis? He didn't know a Judy Davis.

"Who is she and when did she call?"

Kinsley crossed one ankle over the other, keeping her arms firmly across her middle. Good grief. If she twisted herself any tighter she was going to turn herself inside out.

"After she emailed you three times, unsuccessfully, she called Mr. Jamison to voice her displeasure. He called me while you were at lunch, none too pleased."

*What the hell?*

Christopher lifted up the paper with the message and saw a photocopy of what looked like a list of emails. Someone had taken a highlighter to it.

"Did Emmett do this?" he asked, gesturing at her with the paper.

Her cheeks flushed the slightest hue of pink, which made her look even prettier, if that was possible.

She cleared her throat. "No, I did. Christopher, you haven't checked the community relations email account in two days. She emailed us three times—"

"Three times over the course of what, 48

hours?" he asked looking at the paper to check the time the emails came through.

"Actually, it's closer to 36 hours," she said. "I know she was a little impatient, but she wants to give us money and nobody contacted her in a reasonable amount of time. I can understand why she was a little upset."

Christopher watched Kinsley as she stood there, obviously irritated with him. The funny thing was, usually when people nagged him it made him mad, but he found her completely disarming. His gaze dropped to her full bottom lip.

He'd be willing to wager that those lips would taste better than that expensive champagne that Marcos had given them at lunch, and he was getting a little hot and bothered at the realization that he hadn't yet had a taste of Kinsley's lips.

He smiled as he added that task to his mental to-do list.

"I'll be happy to call her now," Christopher said, offering his best smile.

"That's a good idea. The sooner the better. I don't mean to tell you what to do, but you really should check that email account several times a day."

"I checked it three days in a row and there

was absolutely no email," he said. "I've been busy. I know this is your brainchild, but people aren't exactly lining up to leave us messages."

Her brows knit. "Christopher, do you see that piece of paper I gave you? There are ten unanswered messages on there. Well, seven if you don't count the three from Judy Davis."

Her face was so expressive. Those lips were so full. It was mesmerizing to watch her mouth as she talked. He realized he was sitting there grinning stupidly as she reprimanded him. Still, he wanted to laugh. Not at her, but at the situation—at the way the woman had some- how gotten under his skin, but in a good way. A sexy way. A way that made him want to walk over and unbutton the top button of her blouse to loosen her up a bit. Hell, he didn't want to stop there—

"Are you listening to me?" she asked.

"Every single word." He pursed his lips to remove the grin from his face.

Now her hands were on her hips. The stance drew her blouse tight across her breasts. The fabric between the middle buttons gaped a lit- tle bit. He forced his eyes back to her face. And she wasn't smiling.

Uh-oh. Busted.

"Then would you please tell me what I just said to you?" she said.

"You were talking about the messages from Susan Davis."

*"Judy,"* she enunciated. "It's *Judy* Davis. For goodness' sake don't make matters worse by calling her the wrong name."

He looked down at the papers he was still holding in his hand. He shuffled the two sheets and saw that yes, indeed, the message said *Judy* Davis.

He smiled to mask his embarrassment. He never had been good with names. "I know her name is Judy. Says so right here." He waved the paper at her. "I was just seeing if you were paying attention."

She rolled her eyes again.

"You don't like me very much, do you?" he asked, eager to hear what she would say. Of course, he was daring her, and he got exactly the reaction he was hoping for.

She blanched. Her eyes flew open wide, and a look of innocence overtook her formerly contemptuous expression.

"I have no idea why you would say that," she said. "You're my coworker and I respect you."

*Respect, huh?*

But then she surprised him.

"And while we're on the topic of respect," she said, "I need to make sure that we understand each other in a couple of areas."

"Of course," he said. He gestured toward the chair in front of his desk. "Kinsley, please sit down."

She shook her head. "No, I'd rather stand, thank you."

Christopher shrugged. "Okay, suit yourself, but if you're going to stand I guess that means I will, too."

He stood and the slightly panicked and perplexed look clouded her face again. "You don't have to do that. Really, you don't."

"Of course I do. It makes me uncomfortable to have you towering over me."

"What? You're not going to tell me that you're one of those people who believes his head should always be higher than the heads of his subordinates?"

*What was this? A dry sense of humor?*

He walked around to the other side of the desk, careful to respect her personal space.

"No, but that's not a bad theory."

This time she looked at him as if he had just grown another head on his shoulder.

"You do know I'm kidding, right?"

"I wasn't sure."

"Kinsley. We've been working together for what—two months now? I would *hope* that you would know me better than that by now. You're great at what you do. But you need to loosen up just a little bit. This isn't brain surgery."

"It may not be brain surgery, but I take what I do seriously and I would like for you to take *me* seriously."

*What?*

Was that what she thought? That he didn't take her seriously? She was one of the most competent, capable people he'd ever worked with. He liked her poise, he liked the way she related to their clients and of course, he loved the way she looked. But maybe that was the problem....

The Fortune mystique didn't seem to work on this woman who was all business, all the time.

Why not?

Why was she immune when most of the women in Red Rock practically bowed down when a Fortune entered the room?

He liked that about her.

All she wanted was to be taken seriously. He understood. That's all he'd wanted from Deke. To be respected for what he did and how he did it.

"Point taken," he said.

She took a deep breath, held it for a moment and then silently released it. He saw her shoulders rise and fall as she did so.

"There's one more thing," she said.

Christopher gestured with both hands. "Please. Anything. You can talk to me."

"First—"

"I thought you said there was only *one* more thing?"

She gave him that look again, as if she were saying *really?*

"I'm sorry," he said. "I do respect you, Kinsley. But could you please unfurrow your brow for just a moment? Unfurrow your brow and smile. Will you do that for me?"

She stood there for a moment looking at him as if she still wasn't sure whether or not he was joking. He held his ground, looking at her expectantly. Finally, she forced a smile. It was the most pathetic and amusing attempt at one he'd ever seen.

"I mean a real smile."

She put her palms in the air, finally uncrossing her arms. "I don't understand what you want from me. But I'm going to tell you what I expect from you—I'm not your Girl Friday. I don't mind helping you, but I'm not your secretary. Secretaries make lunch reservations. Out-reach coordinators, which is what I was hired to do for the Foundation, will check the email account if it's something you don't want to do. But you have to communicate with me, Christopher. I'm the one who had to deal with Mr. Jamison when he called wondering why we had dropped the ball. I told him we were experiencing technical difficulties with the new email account. But I don't want to lie, and I can't continue to cover for you."

Her voice was serious but surprisingly not accusatory. What amazed him even more was his reaction to what she was saying. He simply nodded and said, "You're right. We do need to communicate better. If you have suggestions on how we could do that, I'm happy to listen to what you have to say."

"Maybe we could have regular meetings and discuss where we're going with the new venture…er, the Foundation's community relations and community outreach efforts?"

"I think that sounds like a wonderful idea," he said, trying not to acknowledge the voice inside his head detailing exactly how he would like to *communicate* with Kinsley.

The woman had asked for respect. He understood that and revered her even more for telling him that was important to her.

"I'm sorry if I gave you the wrong impression. Because you're a very important part of this team and I don't want you to ever feel uncomfortable."

There it was. An almost imperceptible shift in her demeanor, but he saw it. She had recrossed her arms and was still standing there with her closed-off posture, but her brow was slightly less furrowed and her shoulders were somewhat more relaxed.

"I appreciate that," she said.

He resisted the urge to tell her that he knew there was a lot more to Kinsley Aaron than a pretty face and a potentially great pair of legs. There was something guarded and a little troubled about her and he wanted to know who or what had made her that way because she was way too young and pretty to be that uptight.

He silently vowed that he was going to find out. He was going to be the one to teach Kinsley Aaron how to loosen up.

## Chapter 4

Two days later, Kinsley got a call from Emmett Jamison's assistant, Valerie, asking her to meet with Mr. Jamison at two o'clock. Apprehension knotted in her stomach.

Christopher had called Judy Davis right after their discussion. Kinsley had followed up and made sure that Christopher had placed the call. Christopher could be all wit and charm, so Kinsley had been certain that he would win the woman over. She hadn't given it a second thought.

Until now.

Now, Kinsley was nervous that maybe Judy Davis had called back with more complaints and, once again, she would take the fall. Well, she wasn't going to lie and she wouldn't go down without a fight. As she made her way to Mr. Jamison's office, she racked her brain for the words to defend herself if he was calling her in to level the boom.

She loved this job. She was good at it. She'd made great strides with the community outreach program. Really, her work should speak for itself.

When her heartbeat kicked into an irrational staccato, she took a deep breath and reminded herself not to jump to conclusions. Just because Mr. Jamison had never called her to his office before in the year and a half she'd worked there didn't mean the first visit spelled doom.

Valerie looked up and smiled at Kinsley as she approached.

"Hi, Kinsley," she said. "Have a seat. I'll let Mr. Jamison know you're here."

Kinsley had no more than settled herself on the edge of the maroon wingback chair when Valerie hung up the phone and said, "He said to come right in. He's ready to see you."

Kinsley dug deep to offer her most self-assured smile. "Thank you."

When she opened the door, Christopher was the first person she saw. What was he doing here?

He wasn't her boss. Yet he was her superior if you went strictly by job title. When he had started at the Foundation, his place in the chain of command hadn't been officially defined.

But here he was, sitting on the sofa in Emmett Jamison's office. Mr. Jamison occupied the chair across from Christopher. Notes of their laughter still hung in the air. They stood up and smiled at Kinsley as she walked in.

She hoped the convivial air was a good sign. Usually, people didn't sit and joke when they were planning on letting an employee go. She was eager to know what this was all about.

"Hello, Kinsley," said Mr. Jamison. "Thanks for taking time out of your day to meet with us."

That was a good sign.

"No problem at all," she said.

He gestured to the empty space on the couch next to Christopher. For a moment Kinsley silently debated whether she should sit in the chair next to her boss, but she walked over and took the seat he'd indicated.

After their talk the other day, Kinsley had forgiven the flirtation. Maybe it was because despite how incredibly maddening—and flirty—the guy could be, he seemed to have taken seriously her requests to be treated professionally. She couldn't ask for more than that.

She felt him watching her as she settled herself next to him. Okay, so maybe the old dog hadn't completely changed his ways. Or maybe she just needed to relax and own up to the fact that maybe she was the one with the problem. That maybe she found Christopher just a little bit more attractive than she would like to admit. *There.* She'd said it. And immediately blinked away the thought, wondering where it had come from.

"I want to thank both of you for the way you handled Judy Davis," said Emmett. "She called back to say she was delighted with the response she received. I think you charmed her, Christopher."

*No doubt.*

"But, Kinsley," said Emmett, "Christopher tells me you're the one who alerted him to the fact that there was a problem, allowing him to correct the situation. That's great teamwork. It started me thinking that the two of you should collaborate on another community relations project."

Christopher had admitted that there had been a problem?

Kinsley checked herself to ensure that her expression didn't expose her surprise.

*So he'd fessed up... Hmm... Maybe I need to give him more credit.*

"Do you have something in mind?" Christopher asked.

"As a matter of fact I do," said Emmett. "Jed Cramer, principal over at Red Rock High School, told me that you, Kinsley, had lunch with his Cornerstone Club president the other day. He was telling me that there has been an increase in bullying among the students, and he's very concerned. He believes the Foundation can help since we've been successful in reaching teens through our community outreach program. Kinsley, you're really doing a wonderful job with that. I think this is a project that the two of you could really sink your teeth into. Together you could do some real good and put a stop to this bullying problem."

Emmett's eyes darted back and forth between Christopher and Kinsley. "Does this sound like something you would like to handle?"

Kinsley and Christopher both looked at each other and started to speak at the same time. Then they stopped talking and started again at the exact same time.

Finally, Christopher smiled and gestured to Kinsley. "You go first."

She felt her stomach flutter a little, but she ignored it and simply said, "Thank you. Meg was telling me this is an unfortunate reality that's happening more and more these days. The challenge is getting the kids to speak up— not only the ones who are being bullied, but the ones who witness the bullying. A lot is going on here—self-esteem issues, cliques and a general feeling of wanting—no, needing— to be accepted."

Christopher was nodding his head. Kinsley paused to let him put in his two cents, but he remained quiet. So she continued.

"To reach the kids, we have to not only go where they are, but we also have to reach them on a more personal level. What would you think about the Foundation having a booth at the annual Red Rock Spring Fling?"

"I think it's a wonderful idea," said Emmett.

"I agree," said Christopher. "But we will have to move fast because it's happening toward the end of the month. How about if I check into the logistics of securing the booth?"

"That sounds like a plan," said Emmett. "The two of you can work together to plan the approach you'll take and the material you'll use. Here's more good news. We have about $20,000 in the unspecified reserve account. We had a board meeting yesterday and the board of directors approved your using some of that money to implement an anti-bullying program. How about if we make the Spring Fling our target launch date? Does that sound doable?"

Again, Christopher and Kinsley's gazes met. Maybe it was her imagination, but Kinsley could've sworn that something vaguely electric passed between them. For some reason, despite everything that had already happened, it didn't bother her like it would've before she and Christopher had talked. And that felt a little reckless. She refocused her attention on Emmett.

It was probably just the residual adrenaline rush she'd felt at Mr. Jamison's praise. He'd noticed her hard work. She was having a hard time keeping herself from smiling.

"It sounds doable to me," she said. "We will have our work cut out for us, though, with this timeline. But we can do it."

"Sounds like a very worthy project," said Christopher. "I'm definitely up for the challenge."

His words made Kinsley's breath catch in

her throat, which was ridiculous. She needed to stop this nonsense. After her big declaration the other day, if she knew what was good for her she would just keep her mind on the job and stop thinking about how blue Christopher Fortune's eyes were and relishing the times when those eyes lingered and seemed to only see her.

What was wrong with her? Two days ago she had all but read him the riot act about treating her with respect, and here she was in her boss's office contemplating Christopher Fortune's eyes. She needed to get her head on straight. She would do this project and do it right without allowing inappropriate thoughts to get in the way. The last thing she wanted was to let a fickle man come between her and the only stability she'd ever really known.

If her mom had been strong enough to do the same, things would be so different today for both of them.

Well, she would just have to be strong…in memory of her mother.

"Fantastic," said Emmett. "I know the two of you will make a fabulous team. You complement each other. Christopher, you bring the charm, and Kinsley, I know you will keep Christopher on task. I have a very strong feeling I will be calling the two of you my dream team."

*Dream team,* Kinsley mused.

Why did that seem to work on so many different levels?

Over the next few days, Christopher realized just how many members of the Fortune family worked at the Foundation. The organization was run by Emmett and his wife, Linda Faraday, but working here had given him so many opportunities to meet his cousins: Susan Fortune Eldridge and Julie Osterman Fortune, who were doing great work with troubled teens; Nicholas Fortune, a financial analyst who monitored the Foundation's investments; and Jeremy Fortune, who was a doctor for the Foundation's medical clinic. Yet they always seem to have room for one more. He didn't want to be the slacker amid the bunch. He wanted to make sure that Emmett and Linda didn't regret hiring him. He vowed to be his most professional self.

Christopher had taken to heart Kinsley's request for him to treat her with respect. The anti-bullying project Emmett had assigned was the opportunity for him to prove himself—to Emmett, to his family and, of course, to Kinsley.

If he wasn't able to woo her with the Fortune name and charm that seemed to work on every other woman in Red Rock, he would win her over with his new-and-improved work ethic. She was an inspiration. She made him want to be a better man.

He would show her that he wasn't just hired because he was a Fortune. Though she hadn't come right out and said it, he knew she must be thinking it.

The anti-bullying project was a worthwhile venture. It was an opportunity to do some good for the community. After two months of feeling as if he was spinning his wheels, he finally felt as if he had a foothold. Plus, it offered the bonus of extra time with Kinsley. It would be a chance for him to get closer to her, a chance for him to woo her and win her over.

Because they didn't have much time to put the display together, the two of them had been spending a lot of time together. They had agreed to a standing hour and a half meeting every afternoon so they could plan their approach.

He should've known by now that Kinsley would throw herself wholeheartedly into anything she committed to. Even so, he hadn't planned on her practically transporting her of-

fice to his. But for their first meeting, there
she'd been with reams of files and at least a
dozen three-ring binders that detailed the different branches of the Foundation's outreach
program.

She'd brought so much stuff it required several trips to transport it all. Christopher had
helped her carry the bulk of it. Now, the two
of them sat across from each other in his office—since it was the larger space—with the
information spread out across the coffee table.

"First, I think we should figure out what
sort of printed material we need," Kinsley suggested. "I was thinking we could put together
a brochure that offers tips about bullying prevention. Like what to do if you find yourself
the victim of a bully, and what to do if you see
someone else being bullied. We'll need to have
these finished first because we'll need some
lead time for the printing. What do you think?"

*What did he think?*

He thought she was one of the most beautiful women he had ever laid eyes on. With her
long blond hair and complicated blue eyes, the
saying *still waters run deep* came to mind.
Kinsley might seem quiet and unassuming,
but from what Christopher had experienced,

there was a whole lot more going on beneath the surface.

"I think that sounds great," he said. "Do you want to write the copy for that? Somehow I have a feeling you would be a lot better at it than I would."

She had gorgeous skin. He just knew it would feel like silk… He balled his fists to keep from reaching across the table and running a finger along her jawline. She was a natural beauty, and he was willing to bet she didn't even know it.

"I'm happy to do it," she said. "In fact, I already have a couple of ideas for themes. Would you like to hear them?"

Smart. Beautiful. She just needed to know that she didn't have to be all business, all the time. He could help her with that. He felt himself smiling.

"I would love to hear them."

She surprised him by smiling back at him. "Well, the first one I thought of was *Take a stand. Lend a hand.*"

She paused and watched him. Though he knew she would never admit it, he could see in her eyes that she was looking for approval.

"That's great. It's catchy and concise."

Her blue eyes shone. "I'm glad you like it.

I thought it served two good purposes. We're encouraging people to take a stand—that could mean standing up for yourself or stepping in when someone else is being bullied. And of course, the *lend a hand* part is all about helping those who are in distress. My research shows that one of the reasons people bully is because they're allowed to get away with it. When people speak up and then get together the bully loses his or her power."

He nodded. "That makes a lot of sense. It's important that we let people know it's okay to intervene."

"Exactly." Her eyes sparkled, and she spoke with such conviction he wondered if she was speaking from personal experience.

"I'm blown away by how much you know about this subject. Did you research it, or is this personal?"

In the seconds it had taken him to ask the question, the glint had disappeared from her eyes and her arms were crossed over her chest like body armor.

"It's just…" She shrugged. "It's really just common sense. But, hey, I have another idea. Are you familiar with the quote, 'Be the change you wish to see in the world'?"

"I am," he said.

"I thought it would be appropriate for something like this."

Christopher cocked his head to the side. "Why does that sound like something that would be your life's motto?"

Kinsley blushed a pretty shade of pink. "Oh, no, I can't take credit for that. It's a famous saying...."

As her voice trailed off, she looked down at her hands, which were tightly clasped in her lap now.

"I know you didn't invent it," Christopher said. "I was just saying it sounds like a good theory to subscribe to. I didn't mean to embarrass you."

Her head snapped up, and she looked at him with intense eyes. "I'm not embarrassed."

He was tempted to razz her about blushing, but he held back. "Kinsley, you've got to loosen up."

She stiffened. Her back was ramrod straight. Suddenly he wished he would've taken the teasing route.

"I don't know what you mean," she said.

She was fidgeting with the top button on her blouse. It wasn't the first time that Christopher had thought about reaching out and unbuttoning it. But that was a surefire way to get himself into a heap of trouble. He finally decided it was best just to move on.

"Either of those slogans would be good," he said. "Frankly, I'm partial to the first one. I think the kids might relate to it better."

She nodded, obviously just as relieved as he was to move away from his thoughtless comment about her needing to loosen up.

"I saw some rubber bracelets and pencils that we could have personalized with the slogan and the Foundation's phone number. We could have them sign an anti-bullying pledge card. And each kid who signs gets a bracelet and pencil as a sign of his or her commitment."

Christopher nodded.

"That's a great idea," he said. "I was doing some homework, too. How do you feel about some pricier giveaways?"

"What did you have in mind?"

"I was searching online and found a place that offers T-shirts, water bottles and dog tag necklaces. We could put the slogan on them and offer them to kids who stop by the booth."

Her brow was knitted again.

"What are you thinking?" he asked.

"That's a great idea, but it might get a little expensive if we gave something like that to everyone who stops by."

Christopher laughed. "I hope we get that much traffic at our booth. That would show a lot of community interest. But I do see what you mean. Plus, I don't want to giveaway throw-away swag."

"What is throw-away swag?" she asked.

"If it's free, the kids will grab it, but once they get home it won't have any value to them. We want the freebies we're offering to be worth something. So if we invest in higher-quality giveaways, purchase fewer of them and offer them as prizes, they will have more sticking power. See what I mean?"

"I do," she said. He followed her gaze and saw she was staring at his putting green. "Maybe we can use that as the game. Anyone who gets a hole in one wins one of the big-ticket items. We could offer less expensive prizes to those who take longer to putt the golf balls into the holes."

His putting green? Did she know how much that cost? Obviously not if she was expecting him to take it to the Spring Fling.

She laughed. "Now I have to ask you what you're thinking."

"I was contemplating one hundred teenagers with muddy sneakers running up and down my putting green."

"And judging from your expression, am I right in guessing you didn't like the idea?"

He shook his head. "No, not really."

"Oh, right. Anything for the kids, huh?"

"Well, within reason. I was thinking we could have a price. You know, one of those things that they spin, like on Wheel of Fortune. Have different sections with prizes written in each. The kids can spin the wheel and wherever it lands, that's what they get."

"Or they could putt for a prize."

He laughed. "I see what you're doing there. What is it that you have against my putting green?"

"Me? I don't have a thing against your putting green. I just think you should share it."

"Do you golf?" he asked.

"No. I work."

His jaw dropped. *Touché*. The woman had a quick wit.

"Hey, my putting green helps me think."

She shrugged, but the mischievous gleam was back in her eyes. "Lounging by the pool helps me think. But you don't see me doing that during work hours."

"Are you suggesting that I'm a slacker?"

"I didn't say anything of the kind."

"No, but you insinuated it. My putting green

and I, you see, we're really close. It's not the kind of thing I just indiscriminately lend out. I'm kind of monogamous when it comes to my green."

"Christopher Fortune monogamous? I'm not buying it. I'll bet I could make a hole in one before you could be monogamous."

"Is that a challenge?"

She looked at him, the amusement apparent on her face.

"I'd love to say yes, but I have no idea how to quantify that challenge. Besides, out of all the women you date, who would you choose? On second thought, don't answer that. I'm changing the subject into safer territory. I don't completely understand the fascination with golf. Can you enlighten me?"

"Come on." He stood and grabbed her hand, pulling her to her feet. "I'll show you."

"Christopher, I was just joking."

As he picked up the putter, he gave her his most wicked smile. He took her hand and led her to the putting green.

"Have you ever putted before?"

"When would I have time to do that?"

Their gazes snared, held. "Don't answer my question with a question."

He handed her the putter. "Go on. Let me see what you've got."

She laughed. "I'm afraid I might put someone's eye out."

His mouth twitched a bit, but he took care not to laugh outright. He was trying to be careful, going with the flow of the chemistry, afraid he might scare her off if he moved too fast or made the wrong move.

He positioned the golf ball on the tee. "Come here." He motioned to her, and she stood where he indicated. He stood behind her and hesitated for a moment, wanting to wrap his arms around her but instead he explained how she should position herself and hold the club.

When she was in place, she looked over her shoulder at him. "Like this?"

"Not exactly."

"Will you show me?"

Her gaze held his and he was sure she knew what she was asking. So he moved in closer, put his arms around her and positioned his hands over hers, holding very loosely and hesitating a moment to give her a chance to pull away. They were so close he could smell her shampoo…or maybe it was her perfume. Whatever it was, it smelled clean and fresh and edible…fruity with a hint of floral.

He breathed in as he drew her arms and the club back. His body completely engulfed her slender frame, making him feel big and broad as he leaned into her with his chest pressing into her back. He liked holding her so close, feeling her body next to his. For a moment, he pushed aside work and the Fortunes and proper decorum and allowed himself to imagine what it would be like to be Kinsley's lover.

Only for a moment. Then he had intended to dial it back to a safe emotional distance that added up to the respect and decency that she deserved. But after she let him pull back her arm and push it forward in a quick flick of motion, he felt her relax.

He didn't move. Neither did she. They stood there together, him engulfing her and her allowing herself to be engulfed, and the ball sank into the cup at the end of the green.

"Look at that." His voice was low and raspy in her ear.

She turned her head ever so slightly to the left. Her cheek brushed his. He turned to meet her, his lips brushing hers. It was a whisper of a kiss that made his blood surge and his need for her spike. Her lips tasted like peppermint and something indefinable—sweet and female. He didn't stop, despite good sense warning him that he should even if she wasn't showing any signs of objection.

It was a leisurely, slow kiss that started with lips and hints of tongue. Until he turned her around to face him so that he could deepen the kiss. She slid her arms around his neck and opened her mouth, fisting her hands into his hair.

Christopher responded by pulling her in closer. He couldn't remember the last time he'd felt so alive, felt so much need, so much want.

When they finally pulled away, they stood there blinking, both a little dazed and disoriented. Christopher was searching for his words. But Kinsley found her voice first.

"That was unexpected," she said. "Now that we've gotten it out of our systems, let's pretend like it never happened and get back to work."

## Chapter 5

*That kiss.*

She couldn't forget that kiss. Even if she had insisted that they put it behind them and pretend like it had never happened.

She could still taste him. Still feel his lips on hers.

What was she supposed to do now?

Focus on the bullying prevention project that Mr. Jamison had assigned her to do, that's what.

Christopher had been out of town for the past two days. They had managed to maintain their cool and continue with their last planning meeting as if nothing had happened. It was both weird and a relief. They'd kissed. And then they'd acted as if nothing had happened. But that's how Kinsley had wanted it.

Or at least, she'd thought it was what she wanted.

After the emotional dust had settled, she was no longer sure. If she didn't know herself better, she might let herself believe that she was hoping this chemistry brewing between them could morph into a good thing.

Right now, it was a dangerous thing.

Dangerous, seductive and reckless.

Growing up, Kinsley had witnessed first-hand the havoc a dangerous, reckless man could wreak on the life of a vulnerable woman.

If she knew what was best for her, she would get her mind off Christopher Fortune and get her head back into work.

Especially because he was back and they were meeting this morning at Red Rock High School to talk to the kids the principal had identified as leaders and potential candidates for an anti-bullying advisory board. Kinsley had thought it would be a good idea to ask some students to join forces with the Foundation's initiative to help kick-start the program.

*Focus on the kids.*

That's what she needed to do. If she did that, she would be just fine.

All that positive self-help talk went right out the window when Kinsley pulled into the parking lot and saw Christopher's car. Her stomach flip-flopped like crazy.

Glancing around the lot, she realized the only available spot was the one next to his car. She steeled herself and steered her old Toyota Camry into place.

For a split second, she grappled with the idea of parking across the street or driving around back to see if there was anything back there— away from Christopher's pristine new car.

But she let go of that thought as fast as it had floated into her mind.

She was who she was.

She had worked hard for everything she owned, including this seventeen-year-old sedan. It wasn't flashy, but it was clean and it ran well. As she eyed Christopher's shiny red BMW, she reminded herself that she had never been embarrassed of her station in life. No one had ever handed her anything. She'd never competed against anyone other than herself or pretended to be anyone other than who she was.

And she sure as shooting wasn't about to start now.

Killing the car's engine, she sat for a minute, thinking about the situation. She had enough on her plate with work and school. She didn't have time to worry about things that were beyond her control, such as whether she wanted to be Christopher Fortune's conquest du jour. And if the sad reality—that the only reason he was probably interested in her was because he couldn't have her—wasn't enough proof that this game was a very bad idea, then she deserved to crash and burn.

And possibly lose everything.

With that reality check firmly reframing her perspective, she got out of the car and made her way up the path toward the front doors of the old brick building that had housed Red Rock High School for more than fifty years.

A plaque next to the entrance proudly proclaimed that the building was considered a historical landmark and was registered with the Red Rock Historical Preservation Society. Over the course of the years, the building's interior had been renovated to serve modern needs, but the facade still exuded an ageless charm and held true to the history that this town celebrated so steadfastly. Ancient laurel oaks dripping with Spanish moss shaded the rolling front yard, as if they were standing sentry over the school and all the children inside. The sense of history, place and peace was one of the things that made Kinsley feel so at home in this town.

She pulled back the heavy glass-and-brass front doors and stepped into the cool air-conditioned space. Straight ahead, a long hall of polished hardwood lined by lockers on either side stretched before her. The reception desk was to her immediate right.

"Hello," said a smiling middle-aged woman. Kinsley figured she must be the receptionist, Carol. She'd spoken to her when she'd called to set up the meeting with the principal. "Are you by any chance Kinsley Aaron?"

"I am," Kinsley answered. "And you must be Carol."

"That's right." Carol offered a hand. Kinsley accepted it, appreciating the warmth she felt radiating from the woman.

"Come right this way. Principal Cramer and Mr. Fortune are in his office. They asked me to bring you back as soon as you arrived."

As Kinsley followed Carol past the desk and through a set of doors, she fished her cell out of her purse and checked the time, suddenly fearing she was late. But no, she was actually a few minutes early. That meant that Christopher had been even earlier. He might have had a lot of quirks, but habitual lateness wasn't one of them. In fact, punctuality was one of the things they had in common.

Thank goodness Carol stopped in front of a closed door and knocked before Kinsley's mind could continue too far on the journey of the other things she found attractive about Christopher.

*Stop that.* She silently reprimanded herself as a deep voice issued the message for them to "Come in."

As Carol pushed open the door, Kinsley realized she was frowning and quickly checked herself to make sure that she not only had her most pleasant business face on, but also that all errant, inappropriate and un-businesslike thoughts were firmly contained.

There would be no more kissing Christopher.

Not even to get what remained out of their systems.

*What a ridiculous thought.* How had she ever thought something like that would help? Why had she allowed it to happen?

When she stepped into the principal's office,

the first person she saw was Christopher. Her tummy flip-flopped again like crazy, throwing off her equilibrium. Each of her unwavering keep-it-businesslike resolutions flew out the window.

After the meeting with Jed Cramer, Christopher admitted to himself that he wasn't making much headway with Kinsley. Not on the romantic front, anyway.

When Kinsley had walked into the meeting at the high school, she might as well have been on another planet she was so distant.

Christopher was finally admitting to himself that what had started out as a game had turned into something more. He was trying to catch something unattainable.

This wasn't just about physical attraction. It was about not being able to get her out of his head.

This woman was special. She was different from anyone else he'd met. It wasn't like him to be so preoccupied over a woman.

The kiss that they'd shared…and her subsequent parting words about them getting it out of their systems and moving on had plagued him since she'd walked out of his office that day. He'd thought about calling her while he was gone, but he wanted to give her some room. And, truth be told, he needed some space to sort out his own feelings, too.

He kept coming back to the fact that even though he couldn't explain why, he couldn't keep away from Kinsley Aaron the way he had from other women who had gotten too close. Not even after reminding himself of all the problems that could arise if they started something and things ended badly.

He was not ready to settle down. He'd worked too hard to gain his freedom from the ranch in Horseback Hollow to think of tying himself down now that things were just starting to work for him.

But even reminding himself that he and Kinsley would still have to work together if things went south didn't dull this driving need that had him careening toward her.

Since he'd come to Red Rock and started the job at the Fortune Foundation, he'd struggled to keep his professional and personal lives separate. Was he really willing to rethink his personal code for one woman who had somehow managed to get under his skin?

He scrubbed his hands over his eyes as if trying to erase the undeniable answer: yes.

They'd gone their separate ways after the

meeting at the high school but had agreed to meet again in his office—the site of that amazing kiss—for their standing meeting.

Christopher glanced at the Waterford crystal clock on his desk. That meeting was set to start in ten minutes.

He had to hand it to her; Kinsley had a way with the kids. The way she'd dealt with the students Jed Cramer had gathered in his office had been amazing. She seemed to have this ability to reach teenagers, especially the girls, on their own level. By the time they left the high school, she had commitments from all seven students to serve on the Fortune Foundation Community Outreach Teen Advisory Board.

During their meeting today, he and Kinsley would work out a game plan for the teen advisory board, outlining exactly what role they wanted the kids to play.

This had come up so fast, and he had a million things to do after being out of town for two days, but he wanted to come into their meeting today with some suggestions. It seemed as if showing her that their project was a priority might be the best way to break through the wall of ice that had formed since the last time they met.... The day of the kiss seemed to have changed the way he looked at everything.

Christopher spent the next five minutes jotting down some ideas that came to mind. The next thing he knew, Kinsley was knocking on his door.

"Come in." He straightened his tie and raked his hand through his hair.

She walked in with her leather folio tucked under her arm. The knotted tangle of emotions inside him threw him a little off balance.

*I'll be damned.*

For the first time in his life, Christopher was a little unnerved by the presence of a beautiful woman.

How had this happened to him?

Really, it didn't matter. She was here. He was here. They were going to break through this wall of ice even if he had to turn up the heat again.

"Good afternoon, Christopher," she said.

He rolled his hand in front of his body and made a show of bowing formally. "Good afternoon, Miss Aaron."

It worked.

She knit her brows. "Miss Aaron? My, my, are we a little formal today?"

Christopher smiled at her. "I thought that

was the mood that we were going for here. You with your *Good afternoon, Christopher.*"

She hugged her leather folio to her chest and frowned at him. Okay, maybe glib humor wasn't such a good choice.

"Kinsley—"

She held up her hand. "If you're going to tell me to lighten up, just save it. We have a lot of work to do and not much time to do it. We better get busy."

Her voice was neutral. At least she wasn't annoyed or didn't seem to be.

Why was it that none of his usual methods of flirtation seemed to work on her?

Since they didn't, in an effort to keep things light, he decided to quit with the clowning and get down to business.

He gestured toward the coffee table, which was still cluttered from end to end with their previous notes and samples of collateral material. "We've been so prolific, it looks like we are running out of room."

He caught her eyeing the putting green. The thing that had started it all. "Yes, why don't we go into the conference room where we will have more space?" She tore her gaze away from the green and looked him in the eyes. "Plus, maybe we can use the whiteboard in there for outlining our ideas."

Christopher wasn't about to argue with her. He just wanted things to get back on even footing. He couldn't help but wonder if she felt safer with a conference table separating them.

"Sounds good to me," he said. "The whiteboard might come in handy."

With that she seemed to relax a little bit. He had to consciously keep his mouth shut as he forced his mind away from offering her a massage because her shoulders still looked so tense.

Instead, he held his office door for her as they exited and made their way toward the conference room. He was careful to give her enough personal space so that she didn't feel crowded or compromised.

Really, he wanted to make sure he understood the new rules they were playing by.

As he passed Bev's desk in the center of the reception area, she said, "Mr. Fortune, a package just arrived for you. Would you like me to put it on your desk?"

He paused and picked up the homespun-looking package, which was wrapped in plain brown craft paper and tied with twine, glancing first at the return address. Just as he feared, it had a Horseback Hollow postmark. The return address indicated that it was from Jeanne Marie Fortune Jones.

His mother.

A pang of guilt twisted Christopher's heart. He and his father may have had a hard time seeing eye to eye, but his mother was one of the sweetest, kindest women he'd ever known. Christopher new that his move to Red Rock had been hard on her, but he also knew in her heart of hearts she wanted what was best for him.

Unlike his father, who only valued Christopher as another set of hands to help out on the ranch. As he ran his thumb over the paper's rough-hewn surface, he knew that thought wasn't entirely true, even if it did make it easier to justify the way he left.

Christopher felt Kinsley's gaze on him. He looked up to see that she had paused in the hallway that led to the conference room. She was watching him expectantly.

"Thank you, Bev. I'll take this into my office so you don't have to get up. Kinsley, go ahead and start laying things out in the conference room. I'll meet up with you in a second."

Once he was behind closed office doors, he took a pair of scissors from the top drawer of his desk and cut the twine. He used the scissors to loosen the tape and cut away the excess paper, revealing a sturdy cardboard box. He lifted the lid and was a little disappointed when he saw that the package contained what looked like a photo album rather than the cookies he'd been so sure his mother had sent.

He opened the first page and saw a handwritten letter slid into a page protector that his mother had included at the start of the album. The letter said:

*My Dear Sweet Chris,*

*Words can't even begin to express how much I miss you every day. Our family just isn't complete without you here. While I know it's important for you to set out and make your mark in the world, I just want you to know that you will always be welcome to come home when you're ready.*

*In the meantime, I wanted to send you some pictures to catch you up on everything that has been going on since you moved to Red Rock.*

*With all the love in my heart,*
*Mama*

Christopher paged through the album and saw photos of various family members—Stacey and her baby girl, Piper; Toby and Angie's wedding portrait. He lingered over that picture, breathing through a stab of regret for not being there to support his brother on his big day.

The next picture he came to was a snapshot of the Hemings kids hugging his father, Deke. The crusty old jackass was dressed up in a plaid shirt with a bolo tie, that damn cowboy hat that he never went anywhere without perched on the crown of his head. He smiled broadly and regarded the kids with such a look of true adoration. Christopher remembered Toby and Angie mentioning that the kids had started calling his parents Grandma and Grandpa. Sometimes a man didn't know how to be a father but by the mercy of God became an exemplary grandfather. Funny thing was, even though he resented the hell out of Deke for being such a lousy dad to him, he was glad to see the old man showing the kids some benevolence. Lord knew they had been through enough in their short lives; a little compassion would go a long way with them.

An odd feeling squeezed Christopher's chest. He tried to cough, to dislodge the emotion that was blocking his windpipe, but he couldn't manage to make a sound.

He closed the album and set it down on the corner of his desk. Kinsley was waiting for him in the conference room. He'd look at the photos later.

Much later.

Christopher's grumbling stomach was the first clue that it had gotten late. He glanced at his watch and was surprised to see that it was almost nine o'clock. He and Kinsley had been hashing out the copy for the bully prevention brochure since four-thirty that afternoon. He hadn't noticed how much time had passed until his stomach started to complain.

"I don't know about you, but I'm starving," he said. "We've made some good progress here. What do you say we take a break and go get a bite to eat?"

Kinsley swiped the hair out of her eyes and shot him a weary look. "No, thanks. I'm okay, but you go ahead. We're running up against a tight deadline here and I want to make sure this gets done."

Christopher propped his elbows on the table

and watched her as she continued to jot down notes.

"Come on," he said. "You have to eat. I don't want you passing out on me."

Actually, the thought of her *on him* was more appetizing than food. But he kept his thoughts to himself. They had been working for nearly five hours and neither had said a word about what had happened between them the last time they were alone.

"I'll eat after this brochure is finished."

"Even if we get this to the printer by the end of the week we'll still be ahead of schedule. Don't you think there comes a point of diminishing returns after you've been at something so long? Especially if you're hungry."

Her lips puckered with annoyance.

"I'm not hungry. I want to finish my work."

He stood.

"Everyone around here knows how hard you work, Kinsley," he said. "You don't have to prove yourself."

She leveled him with a glare. "That's easy for you to say. But other people around here do have to work hard to get noticed. We don't have everything handed to us."

*Ouch.* Her words cut to the bone.

"Is that what you think?" he asked. "That

just because I'm related to the Fortunes I've had everything handed to me, that life's been one big easy ride?"

She gave him a one-shoulder shrug that was more sexy than it was irritating.

"That just shows how much you don't know. You don't know me at all. So I would suggest that you not judge me until you know me better."

"Is that so?"

"Yes."

"So the guy in the expensive suit who drives the fancy car and has the $3,500 putting green in his office and a different date every night is different from the Christopher Fortune who is standing in front of me now?"

Christopher cleared his throat. "You have no idea who I am on the inside or where I've come from to get where I am now."

"All I know is what I see," she said.

"Well, you've obviously formed your own conclusions," he said. "If you want to go on thinking the way you're thinking, then that's your right to do so. But if you are really as compassionate as you seem to be when you work with those teenagers, then have dinner with me tonight and get to know the real me."

She put her pen down and stared up at him with an unreadable expression.

"So what's it going to be?" he asked. "Are you going to stick to your preconceived notions? Or will you give me a chance to redeem myself?"

## Chapter 6

She should be taking her own car, Kinsley thought as Christopher held open the passenger-side door of his pristine status mobile.

Actually, she should've maintained her *no, thank you* to dinner with him and kept working. But here she was, feeling an awful lot like the Country Mouse who had been ensnared in the City Mouse's grand trappings.

Oh, well, it had been her choice to come. It wasn't as if Christopher had kidnapped her.

Before he got in, he opened the back door on the driver's side and tossed what looked like a photo album onto the backseat. After he had settled himself behind the wheel, Kinsley gestured to the album and asked, "What's that?"

He glanced over his shoulder and stiffened as he looked where she pointed. His blue eyes looked pensive.

"It's nothing. Just a photo album."

"I love photos," she said, leaving the door open for him to say *take a look.*

But he didn't answer, just put the key in the ignition, started the car and backed out.

They drove in silence to Red Brick Bistro, but the place was dark and the parking lot was empty.

"What time is it?" Christopher asked. "Are they closed?"

The clock on the dashboard glowed *nine-twenty-five.*

"It looks like it," said Kinsley. "Maybe they're not open today."

Christopher shook his head. "That's one of the things that I just can't get used to. The restaurants close in Red Rock so early on weeknights. I would expect that from Horseback Hollow, but I thought Red Rock was a little more cosmopolitan."

"Why would you expect that in Horseback Hollow?" she asked.

His left wrist was draped casually over the

steering wheel and his right elbow was propped on the center console. The stance caused him to pitch toward her ever so slightly. Despite everything, she was tempted to lean in so she could smell his cologne.

A lot of challenges came with working with Christopher Fortune, but his smell was not one of them. It wasn't just the cologne he wore; it was *him*. His own personal scent that had Kinsley breathing a little deeper and leaning in a little closer—even though she desperately wanted her personal space. The dichotomy was hard to reconcile. But he smelled of leather— probably from his car—soap and something else she couldn't define. It all added up to an alluring essence that made it difficult to stop everything female inside of her from roaring to life.

"That's where I'm from," he said. "It's a sleepy little town less than half the size of Red Rock. The sidewalks roll up at sundown and there's absolutely nothing to do. Well, okay, there's The Two Moon Saloon and The Grill, but I wouldn't take you to either of those places."

She blinked. "Why not?"

"Are you kidding? Neither is known for its

ambience. They're just not the type of place you take a woman."

It vaguely occurred to her to remind him this was not a date. They were two colleagues who had worked late and were in search of a quick bite. But despite her better judgment, she liked the cozy feel of sitting there with him in the car, with him leaning in slightly, the amber glow of the streetlight casting shadows on his features. Cars passed on the road that ran alongside the parking lot, but in a way it felt as if they were the only two people in the world.

Strange that she would feel so safe and contented sitting in the confines of a car with a man she'd vowed to keep at a distance.

"Where is Horseback Hollow?" she asked, angling her body toward him.

Her peripheral vision caught sight of the photo album in the backseat. It reminded her that Christopher was an anomaly. In so many ways, he was all about flash and being a Fortune, but in other ways he was extremely guarded. That was evident when his brother and sister-in-law had arrived unexpectedly and he'd whisked them out in short order.

It almost seemed as if he had something to hide. Maybe he was embarrassed. Or maybe he was simply trying to keep the Horseback Hollow part of his life private.

"It's outside of Lubbock," he said. "It's about 400 miles from here. Believe me, it's worlds apart from what you're used to."

*From what I'm used to?*

What did he think her background was? She was born and raised in a small town about fifty miles away from Red Rock. It was a speck on the map. No one had heard of it and she was doing her best to forget it. She'd moved out as soon as she'd graduated high school. Growing up with a verbally abusive father who sometimes physically took his frustrations out on her mother wasn't exactly the life of royalty.

Both of her parents were gone now. A pang of regret swelled inside her that she hadn't done more to help her mother. The worst fights between her parents had always seemed to be centered around her. Sometimes her mother would put herself in between her father and her, and that's when her mother always got the worst of his wrath.

In her naïveté, Kinsley thought she was doing her mother the biggest favor by leaving since she had always seemed to be at the heart of some of her parents' worst fights. But little did she know she was actually leaving her mother even more in harm's way.

Kinsley was a levelheaded woman. She knew darn good and well that all the wishing in the world wouldn't change the past. So she did what she'd always done when the past crept up behind her and threatened to take her down—she pushed it out of her mind and looked forward.

That was her motto: look forward, not back.

But right now she was looking into Christopher's eyes, and she knew that wouldn't lead to anything good.

She shifted her weight so that she was leaning against the passenger door. As if picking up on her nonverbal cue, he shifted away, too.

The pang of regret surprised her.

"I have a feeling everything else around here is probably closed or close to closing," he said. "How about we go to Mendoza's and get a bite there?"

Kinsley didn't get out much. If she wasn't working, she was studying. If she wasn't doing either of those things, she was probably sleeping or attending classes to be a Lamaze coach for a teenage girl who she had met through the Foundation.

Work, school and volunteering didn't give her much time for frequenting places like Mendoza's nightclub. This was only the second time she'd been there. The other occasion was for the grand opening celebration nearly a year ago. Miguel Mendoza, the club's owner, had invited the entire staff of the Fortune Foundation, in addition to what seemed like the entire population of Red Rock, to the club's opening night celebration. Kinsley had considered it more of a work obligation than a night on the town. She had stayed long enough to put in a good showing but had left at the first opportunity.

She looked around, taking in the place, as she and Christopher claimed two places at the long, old-style cowboy bar.

It was hard to believe that just a year and a half ago the place had been an abandoned building. After Miguel, who was a former New York record company executive, had worked his magic, the club was all flash and neon.

A pink neon sign behind the bar that spelled out *Wet Your Whistle* in flowing cursive letters. Neon boot signs illuminated the raised wooden dance floor, where couples danced to music that was accompanied by videos playing on oversize screens located around the room.

At the back a doorway with a neon arrow pointed down over a sign that read *Play Time*. Kinsley wondered if the Play Time room still had the pool tables, dart boards, Skee-Ball and old-model video games that had gotten everyone so excited about the place at the grand opening. If she remembered correctly, there was even an old-fashioned fortune teller machine back there, too. It reminded her of one she had seen once when her grandmother had taken her to an arcade, on one of those nights when her mother had sent her out of the house because her father had been in one of his *bad places*.

That seemed like a lifetime ago. She filed the thought where she kept most of her childhood memories, in a very dark corner in the back of her mind where they wouldn't get in the way. She preferred to live in the here and now rather than dwelling on the past.

And right now, she recognized Miguel Mendoza, who was manning the bar himself tonight.

"Good evening," Miguel said over the music as he placed two cardboard coasters with beer logos in front of them. "What can I get for you?"

After they placed their orders—a glass of

white wine for Kinsley and a beer for Christopher—Miguel poured the wine and set it in front of Kinsley, then pulled a frosty mug out of the small freezer and served up Christopher's beer from a tap right in front of them.

"Do I know you?" Miguel asked Christopher. "Maybe I've just seen you here, but I have a feeling we've met before. I'm Miguel Mendoza."

He set the beer in front of Christopher and offered a hand, which Christopher shook.

"Christopher Fortune," he said. "I don't know that we've ever been formally introduced, but I'm in here a lot."

*Figures.* Kinsley did her best not to roll her eyes, but then made herself step back and reframe her thoughts. He was a young, good-looking, wealthy, single guy. Of course he would want to blow off a little steam after hours at a place like this. That's what people with normal social lives did.

She supposed he could turn the tables on her and wonder why she never made time for fun. Sometimes she wondered that herself. But once she finished her degree and had saved a little money...

Then she would start her life.

However, at the rate she was going, she'd

cross that bridge in the very distant future. The truth was she'd never been much of a barfly. That just wasn't her idea of fun. After she graduated she probably wouldn't feel the burning desire to go out and tear up the town any more than she wanted to now.

*To each his or her own,* she thought as she sipped her white wine. But she suddenly realized that both Christopher and Miguel were looking at her expectantly. She'd obviously missed something.

Christopher leaned in, much too close for her comfort. He placed a hand on her shoulder and whispered in her ear, "I just introduced you to the owner. You might want to say hello or something." He punctuated the suggestion with a quick raise and lower of his brows. It was one of those looks that wasn't cocky enough to be annoying. Cheeky was more apropos. In fact, it was almost endearing. She hated herself for thinking so.

"Hello," she said. "I'm Kinsley Aaron. I work with Christopher at the Fortune Foundation."

Miguel shook her hand and smiled. "That's what he tells me."

"I'm sorry," she said. "The music is a little loud. I didn't hear you the first time."

"I understand," said Miguel. "It's an occupational hazard. So since you both work at the Foundation, would you happen to know Sierra Mendoza Calloway? She's my cousin and she works there."

Kinsley and Christopher answered at the same time. She said yes; Christopher hedged as Kinsley did a double-take, but she did her best to keep her expression neutral. Inside, she was aghast. Sierra had just helped them secure some stock photos for the brochures they were putting together for the Spring Fling. He really didn't remember her? He probably did, he just didn't know her name.

Well, she wasn't about to embarrass him in front of Miguel.

"I adore Sierra," she said. "In fact, just the other day she helped me find a photograph that Christopher and I desperately needed for a brochure we're putting together for a project." She glanced at Christopher and saw a flicker of recognition register on his face.

"I'll be sure and tell her we met you," Kinsley said, turning back to Miguel.

"Please do," Miguel answered. "She's a sweetheart. It's too bad. We have so much family right here in town, yet we don't get to see each other as often as we should."

He looked to Christopher. "As a Fortune, I'll bet you understand how that is."

Christopher gave a quick shrug. "Actually, I've only been in Red Rock a couple of months, and I work with so many of my relatives we get to see each other plenty."

Miguel leaned on the bar. "Oh, yeah, where are you from?"

Kinsley saw the look of hesitation flash across Christopher's face. It was only there for a moment before he stiffened and said, "I'm from a small town outside of Lubbock. I doubt you've heard of it. I moved up here to take the job at the Foundation."

"Lubbock, huh?" said Miguel. "I'm familiar with the area. Try me."

"It's a little dot on the map called Horseback Hollow."

Miguel slapped his hand on the counter. "Get out! Are you serious? I have family there. My brother, Marcos, and his wife are getting ready to open a restaurant there, and my cousin Orlando Mendoza works at the Redmond Flight School."

"I was so sorry to hear about his accident," said Christopher. "It was good of his daughter Gabi to come and care for him."

Miguel looked a little embarrassed. "I

haven't seen him since the accident. But I am glad to hear he's doing better."

"You know Gabi is engaged to my brother, Jude, right? She's going to be my sister-in-law. So, doesn't that make us related in some distant way?"

"What a small world. The Fortunes and the Mendozas have always considered each other family. So tonight, your drinks are on me."

"It is a small world," said Christopher. "It's great to meet you. Thank you for the drinks, my friend. But what we really came for was a bite to eat, which, of course, I will pay for. Could we see some menus, please?"

"Of course." Miguel pulled two menus out from behind the bar. "But just so we understand each other, your money is no good here. Money does not change hands among family."

Christopher shook his head and smiled. "I appreciate the generous offer, but really I would be happy to pay. We'll sort it out at the end of the evening."

"Please let me know when you're ready to order," said Miguel. His confident smile seemed to say that he'd already made up his mind. The bill was settled, and nothing Christopher Fortune could say would make a bit of difference.

\* \* \*

After they placed their orders for burgers and fries, Miguel set another round of drinks in front of them and went to deliver their dinner request to the kitchen.

Christopher raked his hand through his blond hair. Kinsley was beginning to recognize that habit as a nervous tic.

"What the hell? Is everyone in this town related to someone?"

She couldn't help laughing at him a little. "Pretty much. If they're not a Fortune, they're a Mendoza and a lot of the Fortunes are married to Mendozas.

"May I give you a little bit of unsolicited advice?" Kinsley offered. The beer had loosened him up, and right about now he was longing to hear anything Kinsley had to say. He could be quite content listening to her read a dictionary out loud because it would give him license to drink her in. He could watch her lips move as she formed the words, study the graceful way her delicate jawline curved into her neck and imagine kissing her at that sweet spot where they intersected....

"Sure." Even if he was in for a Kinsley-style reprimand, he didn't mind. She had a firm but gentle way about her. She didn't grate on him

the way Deke did when he spouted off with his
holier-than-thou statements and rubbed Christopher's nose in I-told-you-sos.

He could tell Kinsley didn't suffer nonsense
lightly, but she was also sensitive enough to
temper what she said so that it didn't feel like
a personal attack.

He appreciated that.

"You would do yourself a world of good to
start remembering names. People around here
get kind of funny about that. It's off-putting."

She wrinkled her nose and something inside him went soft...and then another part of
him, farther south, felt as if it was about to go
rock-hard. He held his breath for a moment to
get a handle on his libido.

This wasn't college. She deserved his respect, especially after she'd made it perfectly
clear where they stood.

He focused on the point she'd made. Remembering names was his weakness, and if
he was going to succeed, he needed to fix that.

He still hadn't gotten used to the pop quizzes
that jumped out at him just when he thought
he had everything under control. All the more
reason that he needed to be on the ball.

Sierra Mendoza Calloway was a perfect
example. Even if they did call her Sierra

Calloway around the office, he should've remembered her. He should've put two and two
together. If he really wanted to make his mark
in Red Rock, he knew he'd better pay attention
and learn the players. He had to know everyone, by sight, right away—especially because
so many of them were apparently family, or
practically family.

Because wasn't that all anyone wanted—to
be valued and respected?

"Thanks for covering for me with Miguel.
It would've been embarrassing if he'd known
that I spent a good half hour with his cousin
and didn't connect the dots."

She nodded. "Well, giving you the benefit of
the doubt, I guess there's no way you could've
known she's a Mendoza. But don't worry, as
long as you pull your weight, I've got your
back. And I know that you've got mine, too."

A strangely protective feeling swept through
him. "Of course I do. We're a team."

Somehow he didn't think she needed his
help as much as he could benefit from hers.
Beauty aside—and she didn't seem to realize how stunning she was—he was in awe of
her strength and people skills. She was young
to be so self-possessed, so stalwartly sure of
herself, yet it was all tempered with a vulner-

ability that made him want to gather her in his arms and promise her the world.

They sat in amiable silence for a moment, sipping their drinks and watching the people on the dance floor.

"So, Kinsley Aaron, tell me about yourself," he said.

She shook her head. "I seem to recall that we had a deal. You promised if I would have dinner with you tonight, you would tell me *your* story. So don't try to turn the tables, Mr. Fortune."

"There you go with the formalities again." He smiled so that she knew he was kidding.

"What's wrong? Does it make you feel like your father when someone calls you Mr. Fortune?"

He almost laughed. "Absolutely not. As a matter of fact, it has pretty much the opposite effect."

"Really? Do tell."

He took a long swallow of his beer, trying to think about where to begin.

"Obviously, you have a misconception that I'm someone that I'm not."

"Are you not a Fortune, or have you been impersonating one for the past two months?"

If she only knew how close to the truth that really was....

"Not exactly."

Thank goodness Miguel chose that moment to bring the food. He set the plates and another round of drinks in front of them.

"Can I get you anything else?"

The food smelled delicious and the company was perfect.

Christopher looked at Kinsley. "I think we're all set," she said. "Thanks for everything, Miguel."

Miguel gave them a salute and hurried off to attend to other customers.

For a weeknight, the place was really rocking. It was great to see it doing such a healthy business.

As they ate their burgers, Christopher told Kinsley about growing up in Horseback Hollow with his mom and dad and six siblings. She was surprised to learn that they had little money and none of the advantages of the Fortune family she knew.

"Are you kidding?" Her wide blue eyes reflected sincere surprise.

"No, I'm not kidding. I had a very humble upbringing. When you have that many kids to feed and clothe, a rancher's income doesn't go very far."

She put down her burger and looked at him with true concern.

"Was your childhood difficult?"

"That depends on how you define *difficult,*" Christopher said. "I mean, we never went hungry or wanted for the necessities. But do you know what it's like to be lost in a crowd of strong-willed siblings, always having to fight for attention and approval, even the last piece of fried chicken?"

She shook her head. "I was an only child. So, no, I don't."

"Being an only child sounds like a little piece of heaven," he said. "But I guess the grass is always greener when you're looking over the picket fence at someone else's life."

He shrugged. "To be fair, I guess I wouldn't trade my siblings. In fact, that was my brother Toby and his new wife, Angie, who stopped by the office the other day. They were on their way back from their honeymoon and stopped in to see me before they headed back to Horseback Hollow."

And he'd screwed that up, too. He and Toby hadn't spoken since that day. His brother had left the ball in Christopher's court, and Chris hadn't moved on it. What was he supposed to do? Toby had clearly come to do Deke's bidding. His sole purpose was to talk him into coming home. It wasn't going to happen. Not anytime soon.

Christopher laughed a humorless laugh. "My siblings are great at making life more challenging."

"How?" Kinsley asked.

"Compared to them, I guess you'd say I'm the black sheep of the family. My little sisters are sweethearts, but my brothers are hard acts to follow. We're just different. I'm the youngest of the boys. They all seem to be cut from the same cloth. They're right at home on the ranch, exactly where Deke wants us all to be."

"Deke is your father?"

Christopher nodded. "Good old Deke just can't understand how I could want more than spending my entire life in Horseback Hollow and working on the ranch. He clings to that broken-down place like it's life support. And he won't take a word of advice from me on how to make it more profitable."

Kinsley sat there with attentive wide eyes, but remained mostly silent. So, Christopher continued.

"Then my mom, who grew up thinking she

was an only child—" he gave Kinsley a knowing look "—discovered not only did she have siblings, but she was one of a set of triplets who had been put up for adoption when they were very young. So then my uncle James, who is one of the triplets along with my aunt Josephine, who lives in England, felt bad that he had so much and my mom had grown up with so little, and he gifted her with a bunch of money."

Kinsley's jaw dropped.

Christopher shrugged. "It seemed like our lives would finally get a whole lot easier. But then, as fast as Uncle James had given Mom the money, she decided she couldn't accept it. She gave it back.

"Every stinking penny of it," he said.

Kinsley was leaning in, rapt. "Oh, my god, this sounds like a movie."

"I know, right?"

"Why?" Kinsley asked. "Why did she give it back if he wanted her to have it?"

"She didn't want to be the cause of any tension between Uncle James and his children. She said discovering that she had this huge family she never knew about was a big enough gift."

Christopher forced himself to leave it at that,

because suddenly revealing his ill feelings over getting and then losing the money felt...selfish and narcissistic.

"But on the bright side, between my mom and her three siblings there are twenty-four cousins."

"Wait, you were just complaining about being lost in a family of nine. How could adding eighteen cousins to the mix make it better?"

"My cousins—most of whom are the Fortunes that you know, or at least resemble what you think a Fortune should be, are a bit more... How do I put this tactfully... They're a bit more worldly than my humble family."

Christopher held off telling her about the fight he'd had with Deke the night he left Horseback Hollow for good.

Equal parts shame and regret washed over him as he thought about the harsh words he'd exchanged with his father that night. But what the hell was he supposed to do? If he'd listened to Deke, he wouldn't be sitting here with this incredible woman right now. If that in itself wasn't proof that he'd made the right decision to come to Red Rock, then he didn't know what was.

Kinsley shook her head. "I can't imagine

having that many relatives. That would just be… I mean it would be cool, but no wonder you have a hard time remembering names. What's your mom like?"

"She is the sweetest person you could ever imagine meeting," he said. "She's all about her family and kids. But I wish she would be stronger when it comes to standing up to Deke. He can be the worst kind of bully," Christopher snorted. "Talk about someone who could benefit from a bully prevention program."

Empathy colored Kinsley's beautiful blue eyes.

"I understand what it's like to have father conflict," Kinsley said. "I was close to my mom, too. Your mom must be a good soul if she is content to build Fortune family relations with none of its monetary perks."

Christopher shrugged. "Are you saying I'm wrong for wanting a different life than the ranch has to offer? As far as Deke is concerned, my birthright is in Horseback Hollow."

"Why don't you go visit your dad and talk things out?"

# Chapter 7

Why was she trying to give Christopher advice on family relations? Kinsley knew she was certainly in no position to do that. She'd run away from problems with her own father, and in the process had left her mother high and dry. Obviously, she was no expert on making things right.

"I'm not ready to go home yet," Christopher said, answering her question after a long pause.

"Why not?" Kinsley asked.

"It's complicated."

Kinsley shrugged. "Yeah, life gets that way sometimes."

She was speechless, listening to this man

who was turning out to be nothing like the shallow, glad-handing guy who on his best days had irritated her…and on her worst days had tempted her.

She didn't want to think about that right now. In fact, she felt a little guilty about the preconceived notions she'd formed.

She wanted to know more about his life at the Horseback Hollow ranch, more about what he'd been like before he'd discovered his Fortune relatives. Even though she only knew a few things about his life before he'd moved to Red Rock, she sensed she knew his heart better now.

*Everyone struggles with something, even if they hide behind a smile. Or in Christopher's case, expensive clothes and a fancy car.*

Her mask was work and school.

She knew that, but she wasn't ready to do anything to change. If she wasn't willing to amend herself, why should she expect Christopher to present a different face than the one he showed?

She had to give the guy credit. At least he seemed to understand how fortunate he was to have been, given a leg up to starting his new life.

His upbringing explained a lot: his need for

attention, his tendency to show off and his penchant for the ladies.

Yes, there was that, she reminded herself. If she knew what was good for her, she would keep that firmly in mind.

Christopher was charming and charismatic. Kinsley was willing to bet that this revolving door of women was as new to him as his red BMW.

Even if he'd always been popular with the ladies, if Horseback Hollow was as small as he'd made it sound, he'd probably never had the smorgasbord available to him now.

Despite that, her esteem for Christopher had risen. She could tell that he had genuine affection for his mother, brothers and sisters. She had to admit that she was just a little bit envious of his big, boisterous family. When she was little, she used to long for a big brother to watch out for her. Maybe if she'd had one, things would've been different. Maybe her mother would still be alive today.

"It sounds like Toby was trying to entice you to come home when he dropped by the other day."

He shifted in his seat and his face closed. "I wish it were that easy."

"I know it's a big trip," she said. "But maybe

you could take a long weekend. I'm sure Mr. Jamison would understand."

As Christopher looked at her, she could see him choosing his words. "It's not the distance. I could fly there and back in less time than it would take to get to the airport. I'm just not in a very good place with my father right now."

"I know there's more going on between you and your father than what you've told me, and I understand if it's a private thing. You don't have to tell me. But logic does dictate that he must be a pretty good man to have raised such great kids."

Again Christopher shifted in his seat. This time he moved away from her and turned his attention to his beer.

"Christopher, nobody's perfect. But please take my advice. Sometimes it seems like the people who have taken care of us will be around forever, but the truth is life is short."

Her mother had been just forty-six years old when she'd died. Way too young. It sounded ridiculous to say—she couldn't even say the words out loud, and she could barely admit them to herself—but it never occurred to her that her mother could die. Her mother, the one who had always looked out for her, the one who had thrown herself between Kinsley and that horrible man who just happened to be related to her by genetics.

Kinsley had been far too wrapped up in her own life, in getting out of the abysmal, abusive situation she was born into and starting the life she knew she was meant to have.

What she wouldn't give to go back and do everything differently. She would've insisted that her mom come with her. The man who had abused them both and cheated on her mother could've rotted in hell for all she cared.

Surely he was burning there now.

But there were no do-overs. She could only look forward and hope that she might be able to honor her mother's memory by helping some other unlucky woman who was caught in an unfortunate situation. More immediately, maybe she could help teenage girls realize that they didn't have to settle for someone who treated them poorly. That by the virtue of being born they were princesses—even if they never had a father to tell them so.

"Hey," said Christopher. "Where'd you go?"

She blinked at him, unsure what she had missed.

"You were somewhere far, far away," he said. "Would you care to share?"

This was one instance when she was glad

she had never been able to cry about her mother and the whole sorry situation. She had always worried that if she let down the floodgates she might never stop crying. At that very moment, she vowed that she would never put her theory to the test.

The way Christopher was watching her she had a feeling that because he had shared his story, he was going to expect reciprocation from her. That was something else that wasn't going to happen.

The music changed to a medium-tempo Blake Shelton tune.

"I love this song," she said. "Dance with me."

She was on her feet and headed toward the dance floor before Christopher could refuse and before she could change her own mind.

By the time she'd wedged her way into a spot on the dance floor, Christopher was right there next to her. Only then did it dawn on her that he would probably hate this song that talked about red dirt roads and doing manual labor.

*Oh, well.*

The dance floor was small, hot and crowded, forcing them into close proximity even though it wasn't a slow dance. But that was okay because the music was even louder over here, and it seemed to keep Christopher from asking questions. Some couples tried to do a slow two-step around the perimeter of the close confines, but Christopher kept his hands to himself and didn't try to pull her into that kind of dance.

Given the kiss they'd shared, he'd proved himself unpredictable enough that she wouldn't have been shocked if he had pulled her close, but this was fine.

Really, it was.

After three glasses of wine, she would probably melt in his arms. She wasn't drunk, just nicely loosened up. Once they had established their dance M.O., she let herself be swept away by the pounding rhythm of the music. It felt good to let her hair down and lose herself.

Christopher looked as if he was enjoying himself, too, moving unselfconsciously to the beat. Maybe it was the wine talking, but suddenly she wondered why she didn't go out more often. Christopher smiled that endearingly cheeky smile as he moved next to her. It struck her that it was a pretty darn attractive quality for a guy to be willing to dance. So many of the guys she'd known had refused to let go like this.

As she took in Christopher's subtle moves, she couldn't help but wonder what he would be like in bed. She hadn't had that much experience, and really none of it was notable, but she'd always heard that the way the guy danced gave a lot of clues as to how he would make love.

If that was the case, Christopher seemed to be proving himself *quite* capable.

Lord have mercy.

She was glad the music was so loud because she felt a giggle bubble up and escape. It must have come across as a smile because Christopher beamed at her.

The two of them got into the spirit, communicating with only their eyes and expressions.

Again, this guy, who she'd been so quick to dismiss, was showing her another side. Here he was in his white dress shirt with the sleeves pushed up past the elbows getting down as well as any of the cowboys in the place. She was tempted to tease him about his ranch upbringing coming out on the dance floor, but that was for later.

This was now.

This was fun.

This was a high she wished would last... and last...and—

An overzealous couple two-stepped right into Kinsley, knocking her into Christopher. He caught her, holding her close in his strong arms. The two of them stood breast to chest, staring into each other's eyes, vaguely swaying to the song's refrain.

Then, right there in the middle of the dance floor, he didn't ask permission; he simply lowered his head and kissed her unapologetically, ravenously. And she kissed him back shamelessly, completely taken by their mutual hunger.

The kiss bypassed slow and soft, immediately igniting into a voracious fire that had her parting her lips and deepening the kiss. Her arms found their way around his neck and her hands fisted into the cotton of his shirt. They leaned into each other as if they depended on this intimate contact for their life's breath.

The whole world disappeared—Mendoza's, the dance floor, the music. She didn't care who was there or who might be watching them. The only thing that mattered was the way he was holding her so tightly against him, staking his claim, in this wordless confession of desire.

The taste of his beer mingled with her wine and merged with hints of the truffle salt from the fries. And then there was that familiar hint of *him* that she had tasted when they'd kissed in his office. But that was then. Now, she tasted a hint of the forbidden mixed with the temptation of right now.

A moment ago she had convinced herself that this was taboo, and now he was kissing her so thoroughly that she didn't want to stop. Feelings inside her that had awakened when he'd kissed her the first time were now laced with a passion that threatened to consume her.

She'd forgotten the once logical rationale for protecting her heart. Or maybe she no longer cared. The reasons had shifted and transformed *why not* into *oh, yes* were promising to be so worth the risk.

Kinsley had no idea how much time had passed as they held each other and kissed as people whirled around them on the dance floor.

As they slowly came up for air, Christopher held her face in his palms, his forehead resting on hers. Maybe it was the liquid courage talking, but this kiss felt right, and the way he was holding her seemed to say he felt it, too.

"Oh, my God, Christopher, what are we going to do now?"

No matter what Kinsley said today, he wasn't going to let this go. They couldn't go back to being purely platonic, not after last night's kiss. They were definitely in a different place now. And he liked it.

Christopher smiled to himself as he picked up the phone.

His gut told him that after he'd dropped her off at her apartment last night she'd probably overthought everything.

He dialed Red and made a lunch reservation for two at his favorite table, then sat back in his leather chair, glancing at the putting green. One kiss might have been a mistake. But two? There was no denying the fire that blazed between them last night.

Even if she resisted, he was going to prove to her that there was something special between them. Something worth fighting for.

He hadn't seen Kinsley yet today, but when he did, he wanted her to know beyond a doubt that last night meant something to him. What better way than to go back to when everything seemed to start—that day that Toby and Angie had arrived and he'd asked Kinsley to make a lunch reservation at Red. He hoped she'd see the meaning behind this lunch date.

He started to pick up the phone again to call her and ask her to lunch, but then he thought better of it. He got up and walked to her office.

The door was open, so he rapped lightly on the door frame.

"Good morning," he said when she looked up from her computer.

"Good morning." Her tone was neutral. She finished typing whatever it was he had interrupted before she said, "Come in."

He walked in and sat down in the chair across from her desk.

"I'm glad you're here," she said.

He smiled and quirked a brow, but she carried on business as usual.

"I realized this morning that we need to come up with a calendar of deadlines so that we make sure we get everything done in time for the Spring Fling. Do you realize it's less than two weeks away?"

*What?*

"That's not what I came in here to talk to you about, but sure. We can do that."

Her expression remained neutral, but her voice held the faintest notes of exasperation. "Would you please close the door?"

Christopher complied. When they were safe behind closed doors, he said, "I enjoyed last night."

She tensed and closed her eyes a blink that was a few beats too long before she opened them again. "About that.... Listen, I appreciate you being so nice about it, but I think we both had a little bit to drink last night."

"We did and it was a great time. I hope we can do it again. In fact, I made reservations for us to have lunch at Red today at twelve-thirty. Of course, it might not be a good idea for us to drink as much as we did last night, since we have to come back and work on these things that you're putting on the calendar." She was sitting there staring at him blankly. "And I had hoped you might catch the meaning in me making the lunch reservation instead of asking you, but…"

He thought he saw her wince ever so slightly as she continued to regard him with that neutral expression. He reminded himself that he had expected her to react this way. *See, he knew her.* And he had also been prepared for the possibility of having to take things slowly as she came to terms with the fact that this was right—and good.

And very real.

"Okay, so why don't we discuss this calendar and everything we need to put on it at lunch today? At Red."

He winked at her. Then promptly realized that was probably not a good move.

"Or if you have a few minutes now," she said, "we can talk about it and get everything all squared away."

He saw what she was doing.

He stood. "Sorry, I don't have time right now. I'll pick you up at 12:15 and we can discuss everything over lunch."

He flashed his most charismatic smile and was pleased to note that some of her bravado seemed to wither away in front of him.

"Okay. Fine. We can have a working lunch."

He opened the door. "See you soon." He left it open, exactly the way he had found it.

As he walked back to his office, he was more determined than ever to make Kinsley see just how good they could be together.

"Hello, Mr. Fortune. It's nice to see you," said the tall, thin, pretty hostess at Red. "A table for two for you and…your girlfriend?"

"Oh, no. I'm not his girlfriend. We're not… We just work together."

The hostess regarded Kinsley with a subtle air that suggested she was just being polite and hadn't been convinced they were even a couple to begin with.

"Well, that's very good to know." The hostess smiled and boldly looked Christopher up and down.

Kinsley's cheeks burned.

*How rude and unprofessional.*

A little voice in the back of Kinsley's mind reminded her that it was a lot more professional than she had been when she'd made out with Christopher on the dance floor at Mendoza's. Anybody in town could have seen them acting like a couple of hormone-driven teenagers who couldn't keep their hands off each other.

Even though common sense told her that nobody was looking at them as she and Christopher followed the hostess to their table, it felt as if every eye in the place was watching them.

Once they were settled and the hostess had managed to tear herself away, Christopher looked her squarely in the eyes and said, "Kinsley, we make such a good team, in and out of the office—"

"That's why we need to pretend like nothing happened last night," she said.

"That's what we said after our first kiss," he countered. "And we see where that got us. Why are we fighting this? I think we could be very good together if you would just give us a chance."

Kinsley's heart pounded an insistent staccato in her chest. It was almost like a finger tapping her chest urging her to do the right thing—to set the record straight with Christopher, to make sure he understood exactly where they stood.

As long as they both worked at the Foundation, all they would be were platonic coworkers. Since she didn't plan on leaving her job anytime soon, apparently that was all that fate had in store for them.

Christopher would be free to fully enjoy all the perks of being a young, good-looking guy with too much money and a tendency to flash it to get whatever and whomever he wanted—like the hostess who had given Kinsley the stink eye when they'd arrived.

Women like that might throw themselves at him, but Kinsley would not be his conquest, and that was at the heart of why they would never work. The two of them came from different worlds. He might think he'd had it bad off being lost in the chaos of a large family where money had once been tight, but he had no idea what it was like to have lost the only person in the world who had ever shown unconditional love.

Kinsley had witnessed firsthand the pain her mother had suffered at the hands of her womanizing father, who couldn't or wouldn't stop himself when it came to the ladies. No matter how her mother had cried and threatened to leave him, he would simply turn the tables on her and somehow manage to blame her mother for his own philandering. Even after her front-row seat for this cautionary tale, in college Kinsley had still been stupid enough to put her faith in a man who ended up proving himself as verbally abusive and faithless as her own father. In her studies she had learned that victims of abuse often unwittingly fell into the trap of falling for abusive partners.

She wasn't convinced that Christopher had abusive tendencies, but he sure did have an eye for ladies. That was enough to make Kinsley put on the breaks. It was clear that Christopher still had oats to sow. She wasn't going to fall into the same trap that her mother had suffered or repeat the same mistake she'd already made….

Last night was her last dance with Christopher Fortune.

# *Chapter 8*

Thursday night was ladies' night at Mendoza's. That's why Christopher was surprised his cousin Sawyer Fortune who was in town for the day, suggested that they meet there to discuss a fund-raising opportunity for the Foundation over a beer and a quick bite to eat.

Ladies' night didn't officially start until nine o'clock, so even though it was nearly eight o'clock, Mendoza's still had the air of a restaurant. The lights were a little brighter than they would be later on, and the music was much softer and less honky-tonk than it would be when the clock struck nine. So they had time to wrap up their business before the party overtook the place. Sawyer would be long gone before then, anyway, because he had to fly to Horseback Hollow before it got too late.

Sawyer was happily married to Laurel Redmond, had been since New Year's Eve. After the wedding, they had moved to Horseback Hollow to open a branch of Redmond Flight School and Charter Service. The operation was headquartered out of Red Rock, so Sawyer still came to town occasionally. Today, Sawyer had been involved in nonstop meetings all day and had suggested that the two of them grab a couple of Mendoza's famous tacos before he flew home that evening.

Whether they were talking business or not, Christopher was always glad for a chance to visit with his cousin because he hadn't really had the opportunity to get to know him very well before his own move to Red Rock. This was not only a good chance to spend time with him, but also a chance to discuss a way for the flight school to make a charitable contribution to the Foundation.

Christopher had asked Kinsley to join them, but she had her statistics class tonight and after that, she was attending a Lamaze class with a teenage girl she had agreed to help.

Kinsley had so much on her plate that Christopher didn't know how she handled it all. But working all day, going to class and then finding the energy to help this girl were just a few of the many reasons Christopher found her so amazing.

She had said she would text him when she was free so that he could fill her in on the details of what he and Sawyer had come up with. She had mentioned that she should be finished shortly after eight o'clock. Christopher found himself glancing at his phone, alternately checking the time and making sure he hadn't missed a text from her.

Nothing yet.

"Are you expecting a hot date?" Sawyer kidded.

"Nope. Not tonight," Christopher said as he clicked off his phone yet again.

Sawyer gestured to the phone. "You keep checking that thing. I thought maybe you were waiting for someone to call you."

"Actually, I'm waiting for Kinsley Aaron, my colleague, to text me so I can fill her in on how you're going to help us raise all kinds of money."

Christopher and Sawyer had discussed the possibility of having an air-show fund-raiser to benefit the Foundation's bully prevention program. Unfortunately, the date of the Spring Fling was too close for them to get something together, but the event was definitely a possibility for the future. In fact, it was probably best to do it as a separate experience, anyway, because it would be another opportunity to raise awareness for the cause.

"Just tell Kinsley not to get too excited yet," said Sawyer. "I need to run all this by Tanner and Jordana before we can give it the official green light. But I have a feeling they will be just as thrilled as I am about having the chance to help with this worthy cause."

Tanner Redmond and his wife, Jordana Fortune Redmond, owned and operated the Red Rock branch of Redmond Flight School and Charter Service.

"I'm sorry Tanner and Jordana couldn't be here tonight to discuss this," Christopher said.

The Redmonds were out of town. That was one of the reasons Sawyer had flown up for the day, to cover some meetings, check on the Red Rock office and make sure everything was running smoothly.

"I am, too," said Sawyer. "Later on, after they give me the thumbs up, we'll all get together and discuss everything. Maybe your Kinsley will be able to join us then, too."

*Your Kinsley.* If Christopher had anything to say about it, next time Sawyer was in town, she *would* be his. Something intense flared inside him at the thought, and the sensation made him double his determination to make that so.

But the feeling was interrupted by a shapely brunette who slid into the seat next to Christopher.

"Hello?" Christopher said. "May I help you?"

The young woman looked familiar, but he couldn't place her.

"You don't remember me, do you?" she said, smiling as she twisted a strand of long dark hair around her finger.

Christopher darted a glance at Sawyer, who was watching them, in the off chance that the woman might be a friend of his. Christopher knew it was highly unlikely, though.

"I'm Crystal?" she said. "I seated you at Red for lunch the other day? And the time before that when you were in with the newlyweds?"

Crystal was pretty enough, but she seemed to have an annoying habit of turning every sentence into a question. Still, he didn't want to be rude.

"Right, I remember. Hello, Crystal. I'm Christopher Fortune. This is Sawyer Fortune, my cousin."

*"Ooh,"* she said. This time it wasn't a question as much as an exclamation. She looked Sawyer up and down, her gaze lighting on his wedding ring. She turned back to Christopher.

"It's your lucky night. I'm going to let you buy me a drink."

Her question-phrasing was strike one. Strike two was calling him Chris. No one in Red Rock called him Chris.

Still, he played along. "Oh, you are, are you?"

Crystal nodded. "Yeah. And if you play your cards right tonight? I will make it very worth your while."

Christopher had gotten used to bold women, but this was the first time he had encountered someone who was downright carnivorous. He glanced at Sawyer, who looked as befuddled as Christopher felt, then he turned back to Crystal.

"Well, you're a very beautiful woman…and that sounds like an offer that would be hard for most men to refuse. But I'm right in the middle of a business meeting here."

At least he didn't have to ask her to leave. She scooted out of the booth. "Well, you come find me after you're done here, okay?" She blew him a kiss and tottered away in high heels and a short miniskirt that didn't look as alluring tonight as they had that first time he'd seen her.

Sawyer whistled under his breath. But it wasn't an appreciative sound; it was more the sound somebody made when they had witnessed a train wreck.

"Looks like someone's celebrating ladies' night a little early," said Christopher.

As he watched the woman walk away, he realized he wasn't interested. Not the least bit. Maybe he had finally had his fill of the pretty-girl smorgasbord. Or maybe he really did have standards when it came to women. How many other men had found it *worth their while* to buy her drinks? He really didn't want to know.

What he did know is that he wanted a woman with more substance.

As if right on cue a message from Kinsley flashed on his phone.

Just got home. How was the meeting?

Christopher picked up his phone and typed, Still with Sawyer. It's going well. A lot to tell you.

She returned, Good to hear. Fill me in when you're done?

He typed back, You bet!

"So, is your *colleague* back?" Sawyer asked.

"She is."

Sawyer took a long sip of his iced tea, then set the glass down on the table. "You seem pretty happy to hear from her."

Sawyer laced the words with insinuation. Christopher shrugged but couldn't hide his smile.

"Yeah, well..." He shrugged again.

Sawyer nodded. "Are you two dating?"

Christopher glanced at his phone again to see if Kinsley had responded. She hadn't.

"Why do you ask?"

"Well, I was just about ready to get on my way to Horseback Hollow so you could *make the night worth your while.* But I'm sensing you're not into that." Sawyer nodded toward the general area where Crystal waited.

Christopher didn't dare look over there for fear of sending her the wrong message. He really wasn't interested.

"It's complicated," he answered.

"It doesn't have to be," Sawyer said. "When it's right, it's the most uncomplicated feeling in the world. That doesn't mean things are always easy, or that in the beginning you don't have to fight the good fight. But when it's right you'll know."

Christopher weighed his words. He really didn't need to explain. In fact, there really wasn't anything to explain. He and Kinsley were in limbo right now, but something told him to stay quiet.

"Okay, then, let's just say, I'm fighting the good fight right now."

Sawyer nodded, a knowing look in his eyes. "Good luck, man. I hope she's worth it. Not to say she's not."

Another text flashed on Christopher's phone. His gut contracted but then released when he saw it was from his buddy Joe.

Art and I are headed over to Mendoza's for ladies' night. See you there.

Christopher considered typing, *Already here,* but Sawyer said, "Are you concerned at all about dating someone you work with? I know a lot of people caution against it, but Laurel and I work together and Tanner and Jordana do, too. We might be the exception to the rule, but at least we're proof that it can work. If you have feelings for this woman, don't let being colleagues scare you off."

Christopher pushed his phone away. "I have to admit I've wondered how Uncle James would feel about workplace dating. She's important to me, but I don't want to rock any boats at work."

Sawyer made a *pffff* sound. "If you only knew how many Fortunes met their spouses on the job, you wouldn't be worried. The only thing you might need to keep in mind is if things don't work out, you can't let it get in the way of anything."

Christopher crossed his arms in front of him. "Of course not."

"Well, since you said Kinsley is important to you, I say go for it. You seem to have your priorities straight and a level head on your shoulders. Just use good common sense."

Sawyer looked at his watch. "It's getting late. I'd better get out of here so I can get home at a decent hour. I'm not going to lie. It's pretty nice to have someone to come home to."

Sawyer reached for his wallet, but Christopher held out a hand. "You came all this way. I've got the tab."

He was relieved that he hadn't seen Miguel tonight. Although it was generous of the guy to cover the bill the night he was there with Kinsley, Miguel's comment about Christopher's money not being any good there made him uncomfortable. He was perfectly prepared to pay his own way. He didn't want to seem like a moocher. In fact, even though he greatly appreciated Miguel's hospitality, he had to admit the thought of Miguel doing so in the future made him uneasy about hanging out at Mendoza's. Christopher's eyes darted back to the phone. Still no response from Kinsley. Then again, his response had been sort of closed-ended. He'd told her he would text her after Sawyer left, which was happening now.

Sawyer stood and so did Christopher. The two shook hands.

"It was great seeing you," said Sawyer. "And thanks for dinner. Next time it's on me."

Christopher clapped him on the back as he walked with him toward the entrance. "Next time, you bring me good news about the airshow fund-raiser and I'll not only buy you dinner, but I'll also throw in a bottle of champagne."

Sawyer laughed. "You better start chilling that bubbly because I'm pretty confident I'll have good news for you soon. Good luck with the girl."

As they were walking out to the parking lot, Christopher ran into Art and Joe, who were on their way inside.

Christopher introduced his cousin to his

buddies and after quick small talk Sawyer said good-night and excused himself.

"Should've known you'd already be here," said Joe. "You get an early start on the night? So what are we waiting for? Bring on the ladies."

Funny thing, for the first time ever, Christopher wasn't in the mood to party. He was more eager to get to a quiet spot where he could write down all of the ideas that he and Sawyer had come up with and text Kinsley.

"Actually, I was here for a business meeting," he said. "It's been a long day. I'm beat so I think I'm just going to hit it." He gestured toward the exit.

"Oh, come on, man," said Art. "Just one drink."

Joe elbowed Art. "If we can get a drink down him, he'll start talking to the ladies and end up closing down the place. What do you bet?"

Christopher usually had a good time with these guys. He'd met them through a local men's pick-up basketball league and they'd hit it off straightaway. Maybe it was just his mood, but he really wasn't feeling it tonight. And he didn't like being pressured into staying.

Across the room, he saw Crystal. She looked

up, saw him and waved. Then she got up and started walking toward him. Even stranger than not being in the mood to stay, he wasn't in the mood to deal with her tonight, either.

The thought actually made him do a mental double-take. What the hell was wrong with him? His buddies were ready to have a good time. And here was a woman who, for all intents and purposes, was a sure thing.

And he wasn't in the mood for any of it.

"Hey," said Crystal. "I see you finished with your business meeting. Come dance with me."

Joe and Art were standing there pretending to be cool, like they weren't watching him interact with Crystal. And Christopher was willing to wager that if he didn't go home with Crystal tonight, one of them would.

"Normally, I'd love to dance with you," he said to Crystal. "But I have more business I need to take care of. These are my friends Art and Joe. Joe, Art, this is Crystal. I'm sure one of these guys would love to buy you a drink." He dug his car keys out of his pocket and handed his friends a fifty-dollar bill. "Enjoy yourselves, everyone. First round is on me."

Kinsley had just finished washing up her dinner dishes when her cell phone rang at about 8:45 p.m. She knew it would be Christopher before she even looked.

Still, her heart leaped a little bit when she saw his name on her phone's display screen. She didn't even bother to dry her hands before she picked up the phone and accepted the call.

"Hello?" she said, taking care to keep her voice as level as possible.

"I hope I'm not calling too late." His deep voice was like sex. The thought made her blush. Where the heck had *that* come from?

Well, she knew where it came from; she just wished she could put it back in its box so that she could put the lid on tighter and ensure that thoughts like that never got out again.

*Remember, last dance. Over. Done. Finito.*

*Good luck,* said an impudent little voice that was probably responsible for unleashing the thought in the first place. *You know you want him.*

"Of course not," she said. "How did the meeting with Sawyer go?"

"The only way it could've gone better is if you would have been there."

"What? And miss all the fun of my statistics class and being a Lamaze coach? Actually, the Lamaze coaching is pretty cool. I'm glad I can be there for Tonya. She doesn't have anybody."

"You've got a really great way with kids, you know?"

She found herself smiling in spite of herself. "Thanks." She didn't quite know what else to say to that. She heard what sounded like a car horn in the distance.

"Are you in your car?" she asked.

"I'm sitting in Mendoza's parking lot."

She hated herself for it, but her heart sank. "Oh, that's right. It's Thursday—ladies' night at Mendoza's." She did her best to put a smile in her voice. "Listen, I won't keep you. Why don't we talk about this tomorrow at the office? Oh, wait, I'm going to be out most of the day. I'm going over to the high school to work with the advisory board and the kids in the Cornerstone Club to finalize the plan for their part at the Spring Fling. I really want them to take ownership of this program. If they do, it will stand a much better chance of taking hold. But listen to me blabbing on. I'm sure you want to get inside. I'll talk to you tomorrow."

"Kinsley, wait. I'm actually leaving Mendoza's. I'm not staying for ladies' night. Sawyer wanted to go there for the tacos. I figured I'd let him choose where we ate since he doesn't get to town very often."

Why was she so relieved to hear this? "Is ladies' night canceled?"

"Canceled? No, why?"

"Well, I can't imagine it going on without you there. I thought you always closed the place down."

He laughed. "No reason to since you're not there."

Against everything she knew was prudent and good for her, she melted a little bit inside.

"Contrary to your etched-in-stone thoughts of me, I'm really not a player," he said. "I don't know what I have to do to make you believe that."

She walked over to the couch and sat down, curling her bare feet beneath her. She was still in the gray skirt and white blouse she'd worn to work. Her apartment suddenly felt stuffy. She reached up and unbuttoned the top two buttons on her blouse.

"I'm not quite sure what I'm supposed to say to that," she said.

"What you can say is that you had as good a time dancing with me at Mendoza's as I had dancing with you."

Her hand fluttered to her throat, lingered there.

"You could say that maybe we could try it again. Say, maybe Saturday night?"

Her fingers pushed aside her blouse's cotton fabric and traced the line of her collarbone. She wasn't sure if it was his voice or his words that made her shiver a little…in a good way… with an anticipation that made her feel naked and vulnerable, that had her rethinking every reason why it was a bad idea to get involved with him.

"Christopher…"

"Yes, I'm here. And since you didn't say no, I'll consider it a yes."

Even though it was after four o'clock, Kinsley headed back to the office after finishing up with the kids at the high school. She could've gone home. She'd already put in an eight-hour day, but… Okay, if she was going to do this, she at least had to be truthful with herself.

She was going back with the hopes of running into Christopher. After all, if he had been serious about taking her out on Saturday night—tomorrow night—she needed to know where they were going and what they were doing, what time he would pick her up, all the details so that she could get ready. She played a crazy little game with herself when she found herself in a situation and was unsure of what she should do—and she still wasn't quite sure going out with him was such a good idea. After all, what happened at Mendoza's had happened by chance. If he picked her up on Saturday night and took her someplace purely social, it would be a date. Even though their date wasn't until tomorrow, she decided to toss everything up to fate: if it was a good idea to see Christopher socially—to go out with him tomorrow—he would still be at the office. If he wasn't there, well that meant it was not a good idea. If he wasn't there she would cancel the date and explain to him that they needed to keep things platonic. She was usually such a practical person that she only used the toss-it-up-to-fate method of decision-making on the rarest occasions. It was like flipping a coin to help her decide what to do on occasions like this, when her head was telling her one thing and her heart was insisting on another. On one hand, if she got involved with him, it could end in disaster. On the other hand, what if this could be the start of something good. He sure had been trying hard, and she needed to give credit where credit was due.

And there was the fact that she just couldn't stop thinking about him.

When she turned into the Foundation parking lot and saw his car in his reserved parking space, she couldn't breathe for a moment.

There was her answer. She should keep the date. And she was so relieved that she almost shook with joy. Before she got out of the car, she took her compact and lipstick out of her purse and touched up her makeup, then ran her fingers through her hair, gave herself a once-over in the rearview mirror and decided that was as good as it was going to get.

She let herself out of the car, feeling as giddy as a girl who had just been asked to the prom by the captain of the football team. As she walked toward the entrance, she contemplated her strategy—she would go to his office under the guise of discussing what she had accomplished at the high school today and ask him about the fund-raising idea that he and Sawyer had come up with last night.

She actually had a spring in her step as she emerged from the elevator into the third-floor reception area.

"Hi, Bev," she said to the young woman who looked as if she was already starting to pack up and head home for the weekend. But Bev was young and she would learn that when you got a job you really cared about sometimes you had to put in longer hours to get where you wanted to go.

*Or you had to come back to the office to find out whether or not you were going to go anywhere that weekend,* said the snarky voice in her head.

In the movie in her mind, she reached up and stuffed a sock in her doubting mouth.

"Oh, hey," Bev said. "What are you doing back here? It's nearly five o'clock."

"I know. I need to talk to Christopher. Is he available?"

Kinsley started walking toward his office before Bev had the chance to answer.

"I don't think you should go in there," she said. She looked around the office as if confirming nobody else was within earshot. Still, she lowered her voice to a stage whisper. "He has a woman in there. And she's really, really pretty. She just got here about fifteen minutes ago. I don't know that it's a business thing. But don't you dare say that I said that."

Kinsley's whole body tingled. And not in a good way. It was more like a pang of regret that was trying to undermine her confidence. She took a moment to put things in perspective. Sure it was Friday evening, but why would Christopher have a date meet him at the office? The woman could be a donor. She could be his sister. He had told her he had a sister. Two, in fact. If she stayed out here when the two of them came out of his office he would probably introduce her.

No, that would look contrived and desperate. A little stalker-ish. Instead, she would wait in her office and when she heard them come out she would grab her things and just happen to meet them at the elevator.

Yes, that plan would work.

"Hey, Kins," Bev said. "Could I ask a huge favor? It's like ten minutes to five and I have a date tonight. Is there any way you could cover the phones for me? Since you're gonna be here, anyway…?"

"Sure," Kinsley said. "Just forward the main line back to my office. But answer a question for me. What did she look like?"

Bev pressed some buttons on the phone, then stood there with her purse on her arm, her cell phone in her hand and a baffled look on her face. "I don't know…really pretty…really classy…like she has a lot of money…like somebody he'd take to the symphony or ballet on a Saturday night. You know, that kind of woman."

"Do you think she's here to donate to the Foundation?"

Bev was already edging toward the elevator. "I don't know.... She seemed to be kind of into him."

Bev pushed the elevator button and the door opened immediately. She backed into it. "I've got to go," she said. "Let me know what you find out. Maybe she's his new girlfriend?"

As the elevator doors closed and carried Bev away, Kinsley replayed in her head the conversation she'd had with Christopher last night. He had said that he wasn't staying at the night club because she wasn't there. He'd said that he wanted them to go out again. When she hadn't answered he'd said he would take that as a yes.

Given all that, why would he bring another woman he was interested in to the office? It just didn't make sense.

Kinsley went into her office, left the door open, settled herself at her desk and waited.

About fifteen minutes later, she heard laughter coming from the reception area. She stood and started to grab her purse so that she could go out and make the *accidental* meeting at the elevator happen, but something stopped her—something in the tone of their voices. Something in the way they seemed to be laughing intimately at a private joke...

She dropped her purse on her desk chair and edged her way to the door. She peeked out, hoping Christopher wouldn't see her. If he did she would just say she thought that she was the only one left in the office and... She looked just in time to see Christopher with his hand on the small of a very beautiful woman's back.

"Our dinner reservation is at seven," he said. "We should have time for a drink before they seat us."

As the elevator doors opened, his hand stayed there as he ushered her in. Kinsley ducked back inside her office so that they wouldn't see her when they turned around to face the front.

Standing there alone in the empty office on a Friday night, Kinsley suddenly felt like the biggest fool in the world. So she'd gone against her better judgment and had agreed to go out with Christopher tomorrow night. Here was proof positive that she was simply one of a string of women.

Her rational mind reminded her she had no right to be upset or jealous. She had known all along that this was his M.O. But she couldn't help the way her heart objected. Tomorrow night obviously meant something completely different to her than it did to him.

If she let herself fall for Christopher Fortune any more than she already had, she was setting herself up for a world of heartbreak. She'd grown up with a mother who had been so desperately in love with a man who treated her wrong. Her mom's love for her dad ended up killing her.

Even though Christopher had certainly given no signs of being physically abusive, his fickle ways, his seeming to want only the things that were out of his reach—and then abandoning them when he was finished toying with them—did not make Kinsley feel good.

If she invested any more emotion in him, she would be mentally abusing herself. That wasn't going to happen.

She forwarded the office phones to the answering service, gathered her purse and turned off the office lights, realizing that fate had given her the answer she'd been looking for earlier that evening.

Christopher Fortune had been in the building, but he was emotionally unavailable.

## Chapter 9

Okay, she was avoiding him.

She had been most of the week.

It was Thursday morning and she hadn't seen him in the office since she'd watched him leave with that woman on Friday. She admitted it was a little childish. But she felt a little burned and very foolish for letting her heart control her usually clear head. She needed to put space between them.

When he'd called her, she'd responded by text—except for Saturday and Sunday. She carefully avoided personal topics of conversation—such as *What happened to our date*

*on Saturday? Didn't we have plans, tentative
as they were?*

She hadn't bothered to explain that if he
wanted to take her out he needed to firm up
plans sooner than the day of—and not parade
his Friday night date through the office.

Even if their relationship was casual, that
was simply bad taste.

Oh, who was she kidding? If she hadn't seen
him with that woman she probably would have
overlooked his lax planning. But it didn't matter now. It was better that reality, the incon-
venient interloper it was, crashed the party
sooner rather than later. Now, she was intent
on locating the silver lining in the gray cloud
that she refused to let rain on her career.

This near miss had been fair warning that
dating someone she worked with was simply
a bad idea.

It wasn't that every man who took her out
had to commit to exclusivity before the first
date. But she realized—too late—that what
she felt for Christopher was different. She
should've known better than to let herself lose
control. Playing with Christopher Fortune was
like playing with fire. She knew who he was
and what he was all about. She knew that she
couldn't play by his rules.

It was best to keep their relationship strictly business. That way, no one misunderstood and no one got hurt.

Monday and Tuesday she had conveniently scheduled herself to be out of the office. With a little investigating, Kinsley learned through Bev that Christopher would be out of the office on Wednesday and today. That should be enough time to clear her head and regain her equilibrium. She was professional and she knew she couldn't avoid him forever. After all, the Spring Fling was on Saturday. But everything was in place. She had done her tasks and had discreetly followed up to ensure that he had taken care of everything on his list.

She wasn't surprised to discover that he had.

That's why she chose to focus on the good, the professional side of their relationship, the part that worked. She just needed to remember to not let herself get snared in Christopher's charismatic web.

She had the rest of the day to collect herself. Because he was supposed to be back tomorrow, she planned on emailing him later today and asking if he had time to meet at the fairgrounds Friday afternoon to do a walkthrough and preliminary set up for the event. They would be so busy with their booth preparations there would be no time for personal talk. Plus, Christopher was a smart guy—he seemed to catch on quickly. Surely by now he understood that their relationship had been relegated to the "professional zone."

She printed out her to-do list and had just begun checking off items and making notes when she sensed someone standing in the doorway of her office.

*Christopher.*

Her stomach did a full-fledged triple gainer, and as much as she hated it she audibly inhaled. She bit the insides of her cheeks hard to get her emotions in check.

*Act like a professional.*

"Hey, stranger," said Christopher. "Just wondering if there's room for the putting green under the tent?"

Kinsley couldn't look him in the eyes. It wasn't very professional, and she knew it. But neither was the way his gaze seemed to be burning into her. She straightened a stack of paper on her desk. She put a few loose pens into her desk drawer. Aligned her coffee mug on the coaster on the edge of her desk.

"The putting green?" Good. Her voice was neutral. "Christopher, you know I was only joking when I suggested you bring it to the

Spring Fling. You don't have to do that if you don't want to."

"I know I don't have to," he said.

She picked up her pen and circled an item on her list.

"I figured we could just have a raffle. The kids can put their name into a drawing for prizes when they sign the bullying prevention pledge card—"

"The raffle sounds great. But let's bring the putting green, too. It will be an active visual. We can use it to draw people in. Oh, hey, and I wanted to tell you that I got word earlier this week that not only is Redmond Flight School offering a couple of prizes for us to give away—a couple of glider flights, which the kids should really love—but also everyone over there is behind doing an air-show fundraiser in the fall. And Susan Eldridge and Julie Fortune were able to snag some gift cards from some of the local restaurants and merchants for us to use as prizes. I'm just blown away by how great and helpful everyone has been. It's a great team, don't you think?"

"Of course. I've always found everyone here to be exceptionally helpful."

"I know. But good teams are hard to find."

Something in his voice changed. "When you have one, you should hang on to it."

Oh, no. Here it came.

She decided to head it off before he could shift things into the personal.

"Yes, we are lucky to have such great co-workers, aren't we? And if you'll excuse me, I'm going to go talk to Hank in maintenance about getting some extra chairs for the tent."

She stood, but Christopher closed her office door.

"I called you on Saturday and Sunday, Kinsley. Did you get my messages?"

"I had to go out of town."

"If I didn't know better, I might think you've been avoiding me. We had plans over the weekend. Or so I thought."

"Well, you should have thought about that before you brought your Friday night date to the office. Christopher, you shouldn't have kissed me if you were involved with someone else." The words slipped out before she could stop them. Now she had no choice but to look him square in the eyes.

The sight of him completely upended her equilibrium. She fisted her hands at her side, digging her nails into her palms. It was supposed to distract her from how she always seemed to get drawn in simply by looking at him. Even now, as he stood there looking baffled.

Wow, not only was he a player, but he was a good actor too.

"I don't know what you're talking about," he said. "I'm not involved with anyone else."

Maybe *involved* was overstating it. "Well, you shouldn't have kissed me if you were even dating other people."

"Kinsley, I really have no idea what you're talking about. I mean, sure, I've dated other women in the past, but nobody seriously. You are the first woman I've even considered dating exclusively."

She suddenly felt claustrophobic. Hearing him say the words but knowing they were encased in a lie made her want to run. How could he stand here, look her in the eye and tell her she didn't see what she knew she saw? At that moment, she realized just how different she and this man who was playing with her heart really were.

"Please don't, Christopher. Don't insult me. I saw you with that woman here at the office on Friday."

Confusion contorted his face. "Nora?"

And now he was going to try and change

his tune, try to explain it away, but she wasn't going to have it.

"I have no idea what her name is, but she is beautiful. You have great taste in women—at least outward appearances. But what you don't seem to understand is that *Nora* and I are obviously cut from different material. Women like her might be fine with kissing and keeping it casual, but I'm not. I don't *give myself away.* Not even a kiss. Kisses are intimate, and I don't take intimacy casually."

She seemed to have struck him dumb because all he could do was stand there and stare at her, his lips pressed into a thin line.

"Since we have to work together," she said, "we have to keep things strictly professional, Christopher. Unlike you, I don't have family who can come to my rescue. My contacts aren't unlimited. I need this job."

Christopher looked taken aback, but there was a new light in his eyes.

"Kinsley, Nora Brandt is an etiquette coach. I hired her because I took your advice to heart. I was thinking about how I needed to get better at learning people's names, and that made me wonder about my other social and professional deficiencies. Nora and I went out to dinner Friday night so she could see me in action."

For the love of God, she wanted to believe him.

"But I saw you with your hand on the small of her back. That's pretty intimate."

"Apparently so. She told me as much when we were in the elevator. Honestly, the entire night was pretty humiliating. I'm not good at this...this." He gestured with both hands, at her, around the office. "I was raised on a ranch. My role models were my buddies and my brothers. We hung out at The Grill and flirted with the same handful of girls who didn't know any better than we did. I have no idea what I'm doing. Sometimes I feel so far out of my element I feel like a total buffoon. So, I hired an etiquette coach to help me. You are so smooth and polished. You deserve to be with someone who is your equal. Someone who doesn't embarrass you like I would."

Kinsley was so stunned that her mouth actually hung open.

Christopher held up a finger.

"Wait just a moment. I can prove it to you."

He pulled a business card from his wallet and handed it to Kinsley. The card had Nora Brandt's photo on it. Sure enough she was the woman Kinsley had seen him with on Friday.

"You can call her if you want. She'll confirm everything."

Now Kinsley was the one who felt like the total buffoon.

"And just so you know, she's married. And even if she wasn't, *she's* not my type at all. There's no other woman in the world I'm interested in right now besides you."

Kinsley had been jealous.

The thought made Christopher smile as he filled the last helium balloon and tied a knot in the stem. Because if she was jealous, that meant she had feelings for him. Even though she was still keeping him at arm's length, the chill had thawed.

There was still a chance, he thought as he tied a ribbon to the balloon and added it to the bunch that would join its twin at the entrance to the tent.

He fully intended to seize that chance and make things work between them.

Today was the day of the Spring Fling. He and Kinsley had met at the fairgrounds early to get everything in place inside the white tents. Hank from maintenance had generously agreed to transport the putting green in his pickup truck. The guy had even taken it upon himself to build a wooden platform to keep the green out of the dirt.

Christopher made a mental note to get Hank a gift card to Red or something else he would enjoy. He had gone out of his way transporting the putting green on his day off. Building the platform was above and beyond.

But Christopher was beginning to learn that was how everything worked at the Foundation. They were all one big family. They helped and supported each other.

After he finished getting the balloons in place, Kinsley introduced him to a young pregnant woman named Tonya Harris who had agreed to help them today. He realized she was the teenager Kinsley was coaching through Lamaze.

Along with their anti-bullying message, the Foundation was also teaching self-esteem. The two went hand-in-hand. If a teen had low self-esteem, he or she might be more apt to fall prey to bullies. Bullies didn't all come in the same package. Sometimes the bully was the enemy. Other times the bully might be the boyfriend who pressured his girlfriend to have sex against her better judgment.

If they could save even one young woman from ending up pregnant and alone like Tonya, then he would consider this program a success.

He admired the way Kinsley spoke to the

teenager like a friend, asking her advice on the placement of chairs and even entrusting her with manning the table where kids would pick up information and sign the anti-bullying pledge cards.

By the time the Spring Fling was open and running at nine o'clock, they actually looked as if they knew what they were doing. Music was playing from a sound system he had secured through one of his contacts. The putting green, which he was in charge of, looked pretty cool on its custom-made, green-painted plywood perch. Kinsley had wrapped a large rectangular box, where the kids would enter the drawing for the various prizes they were offering.

He thought back to Thursday when he'd been talking about what a great team they made. It was the truth. Look at everything that they had accomplished working together in such a short time. They seemed to have the same vision. There was a synergy between them, and if he had to spend an entire year proving himself to her, he would.

She was worth it.

As Christopher was demonstrating proper putting technique to a young boy who was frustrated because he couldn't seem to sink a hole in one, Lily Cassidy Fortune, who had created the Foundation in memory of her late husband, Ryan, who had succumbed to a brain tumor nine years ago, walked up and beamed at him, just as the boy sank his first putt. The kid let out a cheer and Lily clapped for him. After Christopher handed him his prize of two movie tickets and directed him to the table where Tonya could help him with the pledge card, Lily greeted Christopher as warmly as if he were part of her own family. It dawned on him that they actually were related somewhere down the line.

"I came over here purposely to shake the hand of the person who has been doing such a great job getting the word out to the community about the Foundation," she said. She gestured around the tent. "This is just magnificent. It's exactly the direction that I am proud to see the Foundation going. I know my Ryan would've been proud of this, too."

A pang of guilt spurred on by her genuine affection and appreciation stabbed Christopher. He glanced over at Kinsley and saw her helping a kid fill out an entry form for the drawing. There was no way he could stand here and take all the credit, especially when she was over there doing all the work.

"I appreciate you coming by, Mrs. Fortune," he said.

She put a hand on his arm. "Oh, please, do call me Lily. All my family does."

Christopher smiled at her generosity. "I would be honored to, thank you. If you have a moment, I want you to meet somebody who has been instrumental in putting together what you see here, and, I suspect, everything you've heard about the community outreach program."

"I absolutely have time."

Christopher motioned her over to the table where Kinsley sat with Tonya. Kinsley looked up and smiled at the two of them, genuine warmth radiating from her eyes.

"Lily Cassidy Fortune," he said, giving Kinsley a significant look. "I would like for you to meet Kinsley Aaron. She is an outreach coordinator for the Foundation and has tirelessly worked to put together everything you see today and more."

Christopher saw a faint hint of pink color Kinsley's cheeks as she stood and offered her hand to Lily.

"It is such an honor to meet you, Mrs. Fortune," she said. "I'm proud to work for such an incredible organization. The Foundation took a chance on me when I had very little experience—I'm still going to school. Their faith in me has made me want to work even harder to connect the Foundation with the Red Rock community. However, you need to know that this guy right here is doing incredible work. He is making a real difference. He has a great vision and nice way about him that everybody seems to love."

Kinsley's eyes sparkled good-naturedly, but the real meaning of what she said wasn't lost on Christopher. He smiled back at her and quirked a brow, sending a message that she was the only person he wanted to love.

## Chapter 10

Christopher was right—they had been work-ing hard. The turnout at the booth had been better than Kinsley had ever dreamed it would be.

When they started, she was afraid they were going to have prizes to spare. But because of the fabulous response, they were having to tell the kids that they would do the drawings on the hour and that they had to be present to win. At the start of each hour, kids of all ages would cluster around the tent to hear the name of the lucky person whose name had been drawn from the box.

Each time a name was announced the crowd

would cheer wildly. It struck Kinsley that even this was bringing the kids together. There seemed to be no rivalry or resentment from those who didn't win. Of course, Kinsley always made sure to announce that they could win prizes, like T-shirts, rubber bracelets and water bottles, instantaneously by signing the pledge card. Maybe these kids just needed a common meeting ground.

The crowd was dispersing after the most recent drawing, and for the first time since they had arrived Kinsley had a chance to step back and look around. Every single volunteer who had signed up to work the booth had shown up. Most of them were even hanging around after their shift was over. In fact, right now they had a plethora of help.

So when Christopher suggested that they take a break, she only hesitated for a moment. She was thirsty and what she wouldn't give for a bite of the cotton candy that she had seen the kids enjoying.

"Okay, but only if you promise we can go get some cotton candy," she said.

"Ahh, cotton candy. The way to Kinsley's heart."

She tried to ignore the butterflies that swarmed when he said that. She was beginning to realize he was an insufferable flirt. He couldn't help it any more than he could help the fact that his hair was blond and his eyes were a shade of blue that matched the clear spring sky.

She couldn't seem to help the fact that she noticed things like that about him. But what she had also noticed, she thought as they walked away from the Foundation tent, was that he had a much bigger heart than she had initially given him credit for. A lot of his bravado was to cover the insecurities of his upbringing.

She silently vowed to never judge another person until she learned their story. After all, who would've known that slick-dressing, fancy-car-driving Christopher Fortune had actually come from very humble roots? He may have been a Fortune by name, but his modest upbringing really was at the heart of everything he did.

After they grabbed some cotton candy to share, Christopher won her a giant teddy bear at the arcade shooting gallery.

"You surprise me every day," she said. "I never imagined that you'd ever even held a gun, much less that you knew how to use one. You're a pretty sharp shot."

"And that's just the start of my good qualities," he said, wiggling his eyebrows comically. "If you don't believe me, just give me a chance to prove myself."

His free arm, the one that wasn't holding the teddy bear, lightly brushed against hers as they walked side by side through the fair. The skin-on-skin contact made her shudder with a strange anticipation and an emotion that she couldn't remember ever feeling.

"You know what I've always wanted to do?" Christopher said.

"What's that?"

"Ride on the Ferris wheel with a beautiful woman," he said.

Kinsley rolled her eyes at him. "You are too cheesy for words sometimes," she said.

He laughed and and nudged her with his arm. This time the contact was on purpose. She couldn't help but wonder if he'd felt the same electricity the last time their arms brushed.

They made small talk as they made their way over to the Ferris wheel. By a stroke of luck the line was negligible. They were seated and the ride was in motion in less than five minutes.

With the giant teddy bear at her feet, the warm sun on her face and Christopher sitting next to her, Kinsley couldn't remember ever feeling so content or so free. When their car stopped at the top of the wheel, she felt as if she could see all the way to San Antonio. It was magical up there.

The car rocked a little and Kinsley gripped the safety bar that stretched across their legs.

"Don't worry," he said, stretching an arm around her and pulling her to him. "I'll keep you safe."

It was as if they were alone in their own little world. Kinsley leaned into Christopher, relishing how they seemed to fit so perfectly together. And when Christopher lowered his head to taste her lips, she didn't resist. In fact, she met him halfway.

All too soon, the car was moving again, breaking the spell and propelling them back into the real world. The only thing different was that Christopher did not remove his arm from around her shoulder until they stepped off the ride.

She wished that they could continue strolling around the fair hand in hand, stealing kisses and sharing cotton candy. But work called. They strolled back to the booth, not touching, looking as platonic as two coworkers ever looked walking with a giant teddy bear between them.

"You're an only child, right?" Christopher asked.

"Yes."

"How did you get to be so good with kids? You really are a natural. I thought only children were supposed to have a hard time empathizing with others. And that was supposed to be a joke but it didn't come out very well."

She smiled as he pretended to knock himself up the side of his head with the palm of his hand. "Just because I was an only child doesn't mean I can't relate to people, Christopher."

"What I'm trying so ineloquently to say is that I love watching you with the kids. They really listen to you and respect you. I think kids have a natural B.S. meter. They can tell when someone is sincere and when they're not. You're really good at what you do."

Her natural inclination was to make a joke out of his compliment or to spit out some snarky retort. But the words got caught in her throat. All she could manage was a choked "Thank you."

She cleared her throat. "I feel so lucky to do what I do, to have a job where I have an opportunity to make a real difference."

Christopher smiled. "Only-child anomaly number two—you're not selfish, either."

She felt her cheeks warming. "Would you stop with the compliments, already?" She shot him a smile so that he knew she was kidding. "Thank you. But good grief, if you keep this up my head is going to swell as big as the bouncy castle over in the kids' area."

"If it does, you'll have good reason."

"Christopher…"

"How did you meet Tonya?"

She smiled at the mention of the sweet teenage girl. "I met her at the high school a few months ago when I was there doing a presentation for Principal Cramer. She had just found out she was pregnant. Her parents had kicked her out of the house, and she really didn't have anywhere else to go. The boyfriend lives over in San Antonio and dumped her as soon as he found out they were going to be parents. She had slept at the bus station the night before and had almost gotten on a bus to San Antonio to try to talk to the boyfriend. The only thing that stopped her was that she didn't have enough money for a ticket. She went to school the next day because she didn't have any place else to go. I feel like it was divine intervention that I was there for her."

Christopher raked his hand through his hair. It wasn't a gesture of vanity as much as what seemed to be an expression of disbelief. The astonishment in his eyes spoke volumes.

"She broke down that day and cried and cried, right in my arms. I cried with her. And then I told her that she was allowed to have a twenty-four-hour pity party, but after that she needed to be strong for both her sake and the baby's. She stayed at my apartment that night and I went with her to talk to her parents the next day. They let her come back and that's where she is now. Her grades are good and she'll miss a little school when she has the baby in about three months, but I've already talked to the principal and we've arranged for her to do schoolwork while she's out. Her mother is going to watch the baby during the day, and she might have to get an after-school job to afford diapers, but she should be okay. I just keep telling her the most important thing is that she can't get behind on her schoolwork and she can't just give up. If she doesn't, everything will be fine."

Kinsley shrugged at a loss for what else to say.

"Isn't that what everybody needs sometimes?" Christopher said. "For somebody to tell them that they can do it? That the road ahead may be hard, but if they're persistent everything will be fine. Kinsley, you may have saved that girl's life. You helped her smooth things over with her family so that she has the support she needs until she graduates and gets a full-time job."

She didn't know what to say. So she didn't say anything for a long while as they walked. Then she identified one of the feelings knotted in her belly. It was shame.

"I meant what I said to Lily Fortune earlier. You really have done a good job. I didn't give you enough credit when you first started. I thought you were just trading on your name and your good looks."

"Oh, well, you've got to cut a guy a break in the trading-on-his-looks department." He shrugged and did a Justin Bieber-ish shake of his head, despite the fact that his close-cropped hair didn't move.

She knew he was kidding, but she couldn't resist egging him on. "And here I thought you were the humble Fortune—"

Her words were eclipsed by a commotion coming from the Foundation tent. She and Christopher exchanged a concerned glance and jogged over to the tent to see what was happening.

A sluggish-looking teenage boy was standing in an aggressive pose over Tonya, who was still seated at the table. The two were exchanging heated words. When Tonya stood and backed away from the guy, he reached out a hand, grabbed the back of her T-shirt and pulled hard. Tonya stumbled and immediately put her hands up, as if to shield herself from a blow. That's all it took for Kinsley to break into a sprint and put herself between Tonya and the boy.

"What the heck do you think you're doing?" she said to the guy. She got right in his face, determined to prove that she wasn't afraid of him. She looked the thug square in the eyes but kept her voice level and low as she spoke with authority. "You need to leave now. *Now.* Or I am going to call the police and have them escort you out of here."

A cocky sneer spread slowly over the guy's face. He was tall, but he was skinny. And although she didn't want to lay a hand on him, she was perfectly prepared to practice a few self-defense moves that she had learned over the years.

"I'm just here to talk to my baby mama," he said.

"It didn't look like you were talking to her. It looked like you were upsetting her."

"I don't need you interfering with me and my family," the thug said.

Kinsley sneered right back at him. "Oh, then you must be Jared. I've heard about you, Jared."

The kid seemed to flinch at the revelation that Kinsley knew him. "I think Tonya's dad would like to have a conversation with you. In fact, he's supposed to be stopping by any minute. Why don't you have a seat over there and wait for them?"

Kinsley could honestly say it was the first time she had seen all the blood drain from a person's face. Jared didn't say another word. He turned and sprinted away. It was only then that Kinsley realized that Christopher was standing right next to her, looking as if he was ready to spring into action if Jared had made one false move.

He squeezed her arm. "Why don't you see to Tonya? I'll deal with the crowd." He motioned with his head to the knot of onlookers that had gathered to watch the confrontation.

"Thank you," she said, giving him a squeeze back.

Tonya was huddled in the far corner of the tent, sobbing.

"Honey, I'm so sorry. Did he hurt you?"

Tonya shook her head as tears streamed down her face.

"What did he want?" Kinsley asked this question only to find out if Jared had been coming around other times or if this happened to be a chance encounter.

"Nothing," Tonya said. "He was just being disgusting. He's here at the Spring Fling with his buddies and he just wanted to act like a jerk."

And nobody had stepped in to help her.

"How long had you been standing there before I got back?"

Tonya shrugged as she swiped at her tears. Kinsley reached into her pocket and handed the girl a tissue. The girl blew her nose.

"He first saw me about ten minutes after you'd gone on break. He and his friends came up to me. I thought he wanted to say hi, but he called me a whore, asked me why I was here. He said they didn't allow whores at the Spring Fling. Then he walked away laughing with his friends. He came back just before you did."

Kinsley's mouth went dry.

"I'm so sorry this happened. But I don't think he's going to bother you anymore. If he does, you need to tell someone."

A dozen questions darted through her

mind—at the top of the list was whether this was the first time she'd seen him since she told him about the baby and whether he had ever hit her in the past. His aggressive posture and Tonya's reaction made Kinsley wonder, but now wasn't the time to ask her. She gathered Tonya in her arms and let her cry on her shoulder, gently patting her on the back the same way she had the first day they'd met.

When Tonya's father arrived, she would let him know that Jared had been hassling her.

The girl needed to know she didn't have to put up with that kind of treatment. She needed to know she deserved better. Once she had calmed down, they would talk about that.

But there was one thing she needed to know right now. "Sweetie, did anyone try to help you? Did anyone tell him to go away?"

"No."

That was the crux of the matter. That's why they needed to educate people about taking a stand to help others. Kinsley focused on the clinical side of it because if she thought about all those people standing there looking on and no one caring enough to get involved, she would be sobbing as hard as Tonya was. How could people be so heartless? To stand there while an innocent girl was being verbally attacked. Who knows what might have happened if she and Christopher hadn't come back when they did.

She squeezed her eyes shut to dam the tears that were welling and to try and erase the image of her father swinging and hitting her mother when she had jumped between them, just as she had jumped between Tonya and Jared.

A few hours later, it was time for the Spring Fling to close. The booth was empty except for Christopher and Kinsley. Tonya's father had come to get her as soon as Kinsley had called him. She had sent home all of her volunteers after they had put in such a long day's work. There wasn't much to break down now, only the chairs and the tables, which they just needed to fold up and set aside so that Hank could come by tomorrow morning and load them along with the tent into his truck.

"What did Tonya's father say?" Christopher asked.

Christopher kept a respectable distance when Mr. Harris had come by to collect his daughter.

"He said he was going to talk to the sheriff about a restraining order," Kinsley said. "I think that's a good idea."

Her voice cracked on the last words. It was probably the combination of fatigue and the letdown after the adrenaline rush, but suddenly all the tears that she'd been able to contain while she was comforting Tonya threatened to break through. If they did, she was afraid she might not stop crying.

"You were the epitome of grace under pressure," Christopher said.

Kinsley opened her mouth to say, "No," but the words lodged in her throat as tears broke free and rolled down her cheek. She turned her head, hoping that Christopher wouldn't see.

"Hey—" he said, putting a gentle hand on her shoulder. "Everything is going to be okay."

She wished she could believe him, but for girls like Tonya and for women like her mother, nothing ever turned out okay. The tears crested and streamed. The harder she tried to stop them, the harder she cried.

The tables and chairs could wait.

Kinsley could not.

Christopher had to get her out of there and to a place where she felt safe enough to let out whatever it was that had her so tied up in knots. The episode with Tonya and Jared was upsetting, but she'd handled it well. However, it had obviously brought up something else.

He hoped she would let down her walls and trust him enough to let him help her.

He saw two boys who had been helping at the Foundation tent that afternoon. Now they were just hanging around. He offered to pay them twenty dollars each if they would stack the chairs and break down the tables and leave them over by the tree. The two jumped at the chance to make an easy buck, freeing Kinsley and him to leave.

She seemed much too upset to drive, so Christopher was relieved when she allowed him to take her home. He told her he would pick her up in the morning and they would come and get her car then. Just to ease her mind, he phoned the fairgrounds security office and informed them they would be back to get the car tomorrow.

By the time they had gotten to her apartment, Kinsley had composed herself. Even so, he tenderly helped her upstairs, but just as he expected, once they were inside, she tried to downplay what happened.

The walls were firmly back in place.

"Kinsley, you don't have to do this with me," Christopher insisted. "You're not an island. You don't have to go this alone—whatever it is that is torturing you. Haven't we gone beyond that?"

He reached out and tucked a strand of hair behind her ear.

"Talk to me," he said.

She was silent for a moment as they sat together on the couch. Christopher was determined to not fill the silence. It worked.

"I told you that both of my parents are dead," Kinsley said in a small voice.

Christopher nodded.

"It was my father's doing. Well, mostly. He drank himself to death, and my mother never recovered. It's as if she died from a broken heart. Not because she loved him. Her heart broke because of the way he had treated her. He was the quintessential bully, made her believe that she was worthless. No one should have to live that way."

Listening to the words, Christopher felt all the blood drain from his face. He reached out and took Kinsley's hand in silent support.

"I couldn't do anything to help her," she said. "I guess I thought she would heal, that her life would get better after he was gone. But she didn't, she just wasted away. And died. As I was growing up, as far back as I can remember my father always belittled my mother, and she was defenseless against his words— and sometimes his fists. He had such an anger problem. He thought I had a smart mouth when I would stand up for her, so he'd come at me, and my mother would put herself between us and bear the brunt of his anger so that I could get away. She just let him treat her that way."

He squeezed her hand and shut his eyes for a moment. When he opened them, he said, "Kinsley, I am so sorry."

She shook her head. "Please don't feel sorry for me. I don't want anyone's pity. Sure I wish I could've done things differently. I wish I could go back and force my mom to move out, to get away from him, but I can't and I know that. I made a decision long ago, Christopher, not to let my past define me. But it does inform my choices."

"Is that why you were so quick to put your-self in between Tonya and Jared?"

*And why you tend to keep people at arm's length.*

She nodded.

He pulled her into his arms and held her, just held her, for the longest time.

"I am so sorry for what you went through," he whispered in her ear. "But I'm not sorry for

who you've become. You are one of the stron-
gest, most amazing people I have ever met in
my entire life."

He leaned his head in so that his cheek was
on hers. The next thing he knew her mouth,
soft, warm and inviting, had found his.

It vaguely registered that he shouldn't be
doing this—she was vulnerable right now. But
he was kissing her and she was kissing him
back.

Her lips tortured and tempted him more than
they satisfied his craving for her. As he sat
there with his arms around her, the feel of her
lips on his urged him to lean in closer. Raw
need swirled inside him, as if taking possession of her might bind them and fix everything
that was broken.

A moan deep in his throat escaped as desire coursed through him, a yearning only in-
tensified by the feel of her lips. His one lucid
thought as Kinsley melted into him was the
taste of her: sweet as spun sugar and candy
apples and something warm…like cinnamon
and sunshine.

It made him reel.

For a few glorious seconds he never wanted
to breathe on his own again. He could be per-

fectly content right here with her in his arms
for the rest of his life.

His hands slid down to her waist and held
her firmly against him as his need for her grew
and pulsed.

He slowly released her, staying forehead
to forehead while the heat between them lingered, drawing him to her almost magnetically.
He reached out and ran the pad of his thumb
over her bottom lip.

"I'd better go," he whispered. "If I don't…
you know what's bound to happen."

"I know," she said. "And I want you to stay."

Caught in the twilight between craving and
clarity, he claimed one more kiss of her lips
but knew this was as far as they should go. As
much as he wanted her, it wouldn't be right.

"I don't want to force things," he said, his
lips still a breath away from hers.

"You and I both know we've been moving
toward this moment for weeks—for months,"
she said. "Probably since the first moment we
saw each other."

Her words, the nearness of her, sent heat rip-
pling through his body. As she gently nipped
at his bottom lip, he had to fight the desire to
take her right there, right now, but in a way that
would reach back through space and time and

make right all the wrongs and ugliness that had ever darkened her world.

Tonight felt different.

This *thing* between them felt deeper and undeniably right. For the first time in a long time—maybe ever—his heart was no longer his own. Her essence had infused his senses. All the Fortunes' money couldn't buy what he'd found in her.

Then those lips that had been driving him crazy took possession of his once again, and he knew there was no turning back from what was about to happen.

They were inevitable.

## Chapter 11

Kinsley got to her feet and took Christopher's hand. If this was going to happen, she was going to have to prove to him she wasn't simply seeking sanctuary in his body. She needed to show him that she was truly ready.

She led him to the bedroom.

It had been a long time since she'd allowed herself to fully want, to fully trust, but all that mattered was how she needed this man. His evident need for her made her feel powerful and desirable. Strong and beautiful. No one had ever made her feel like this before.

Piece by piece their clothes fell away until they stood naked in front of each other in the dim light of the bedroom lit by moonlight filtering in through the sheer curtains. His gaze searched her face as if he were giving her one last chance to protest.

Not a chance.

As if reading her mind, he walked her backward to the bed and lowered her onto it. Climbing in beside her, he stretched out, propping his head on his free hand to look into her eyes.

She rolled over to face him so that their lips were a whisper away. She wanted him to see that this was exactly what she wanted. He reached out and smoothed her hair away from her face, then traced a finger down to her breasts. He smoothed his palm over the sensitive skin, making her inhale sharply.

"You are so beautiful," he said. "I can't tell you how long I've wanted this...wanted us."

He closed the distance between them, allowing no room for doubt. Her lips were still swollen and tender from kissing him earlier, but still she opened her mouth to let him all the way in.

He responded by rolling her onto her back and gently nudging her legs apart. He covered her with his body as she ran her hands down his arms, then up his back as he settled himself on her, positioning himself so that his hips were square to hers. The feel of him on top of her released all the desire and longing that had been bottling up in her since the day she'd first realized that she wanted him.

She tried to stifle a groan that bubbled up in her throat as she savored the heat that coursed between them. She reveled in the feel of him, in the anticipation of the imminent joining of their bodies.

It had been such a long time since she'd felt this way about anyone, since she'd allowed herself to lose control and trust someone like she trusted him.

It was good that they'd talked tonight, that she'd opened up to him. It was cathartic, as if trusting him with her past had cleared a path to the future.

She wasn't sure what was going to happen after tonight, but she wasn't going to think about that now. All she cared about was the tender way he was kissing her neck as she lolled her head to the side to give him easier access. Now, his lips were trailing a path over her collarbones, then dipping down into the valley between her breasts.

One thing she had learned from Christopher was that you had to seize every moment, every opportunity and live. Until now, she hadn't been able to do that. But tonight she was in the here and now. Tonight, she intended to make love to him as if there would never be another moment like this one.

His kisses had found their way to her abdomen and were circling her belly button. Then he took a detour and kissed the insides of her thighs. She inhaled sharply and her eyes widened.

"Why did we wait so long for this?" Her voice was soft and breathless in the darkness.

"I don't know, but I can promise you it will be worth the wait." He flashed a wicked smile at her as he climbed back toward her. With a firm, quick move he pulled her on top of him. She could feel the hard length of him and she had to fight the urge to slide her body down and take him inside of her.

She drew in a jagged breath, determined to not rush things. Determined to savor every last delicious second of their first time together.

"But if you've changed your mind, I can stop," he said. "Are you sure about this?"

She nodded, then kissed him lightly on the mouth.

"I want you so badly, I can't think of anything else. So, if you're sure, then—"

*"Shhh..."* She pressed her finger to his lips.

"I'm sure. Kiss me. Make love to me. Let's let what's in the past stay in the past. We can worry about tomorrow...tomorrow. Because tonight, I'm really glad we're right here."

He kissed her softly, then he slowly spread his hands over her breasts before gently cupping them. She was beautiful, all curves and legs and porcelain skin. He marveled at the ivory breasts in his hands and reverently closed his mouth over a nipple.

The sound of her sigh made him want her all the more.

He stretched out on top of her, gently nudging her legs apart with his knee. But then he felt her stiffen. She bit her lip and looked at him as if there was something she needed to say but couldn't find the words.

Had she changed her mind?

"What's wrong?" he asked, smoothing the back of his hand over her cheek.

She bit her bottom lip. "It's been a long time since I've been with anyone. So I'm not on birth control."

He bit back a curse. How could he have been so damn stupid? He was always cautious. He never had unprotected sex. It was a chance he wouldn't take for so many different reasons. Reasons that could justify a whole new division at the Foundation. Yet, tonight, being here with her so unexpectedly…wanting her as badly as he did, he'd pushed toward this coupling without thinking things through. Mainly because he hadn't been so presumptuous to think that he'd find himself in her bed.

"Oh…well…wow." He pulled himself off her and shifted onto his side so that he could look at her. He definitely needed some space, some room to cool off. "I don't have anything, either."

He cursed silently for not being prepared because he wanted her so much it almost caused him physical pain. He hoped it didn't show on his face as he stared into her beautiful, tormented blue eyes.

As she lay there illuminated by the moonlight filtering in through the slats in the plantation shutters, he realized he'd probably never seen her look quite so beautiful. That's when he knew…being here with her like this…holding her, feeling the warmth of her against him was all he needed.

"We don't have to make love tonight. We can just hold each other…or do other things. I can pick up some condoms tomorrow."

\* \* \*

Never in her life had she experienced the perfect blend of euphoria and disappointment.

Euphoria because Christopher didn't have protection ready and waiting in his wallet or wherever grown men kept them these days. It meant that he wasn't prepared for a spur of the moment encounter, which put her mind at ease, and it showed that he cared about her and about his own health. He wasn't willing to have unprotected sex.

But she was also disappointed because she wanted him so badly that she... Okay, now she was blushing.

"So, here we are," he said, drawing in a deep breath. Clearly, this sudden one hundred miles per hour to zero stop was just as jarring for him as it was for her.

He made a pained noise as he adjusted his position on the bed.

"So, here we are," she said.

He raked his hand through his hair. "Not to bring up a sore subject, but does this prove to you that I'm not as big a player as you think I am?"

She ran her fingers over the hair on his chest. His perfectly natural chest was almost as sexy as his broad shoulders, which she touched appreciatively.

"Honey, if I still believed you were a player, you wouldn't be here naked in my bed."

"Touché."

He looked almost edible lying there propped up on his side, watching her with his sexy eyes. She didn't feel the need to cover up or hide from him. In fact, she loved the fact that, judging by his body language, he obviously liked what he saw.

"So I gather you must not have been a Boy Scout," she said.

He grinned. "Ahh, because I'm not prepared." He laughed. "Actually, I *was* a Scout, way back when. I guess I'm a bit rusty in the preparedness department these days. But don't tell anyone because I may have to give back my merit badge."

"You can always earn that badge back."

"Oh, yeah? Exactly what did you have in mind?"

She ran her hand down the length of his body until she found his manhood. She touched him, happy to see that he was still every bit as ready to go as he had been before they'd been forced to stop.

"How do you feel about going and getting

something for us? There's a twenty-four-hour drugstore two blocks from here. Will you do it? Please?"

He pursed his lips, and at first he seemed uncertain. For a moment she thought he might say no. But then he leaned in and feathered a kiss onto her lips before he lifted himself off the bed and got dressed.

He was back within ten minutes.

While he was gone, Kinsley opened a bottle of wine and lit some candles.

She handed him a glass when he came into the bedroom. "I was going to say that this deed deserved another kind of merit badge," he said as he sat on the edge of the bed, "but I see that you're way ahead of me."

She smiled. "So kiss me."

He complied, kissing her for a long time. Leisurely and thorough kisses that had her wondering, once again, if he had changed his mind while he was out and decided to take things slowly. He was still dressed even though he was stretched out beside her on the bed.

She ran her hand along the waistband of his blue jeans, tearing at the fabric of his shirt until her fingers struck gold...bare skin. He helped her by drawing it up and over his head.

She sighed as she drank in the raw beauty of

him. When she straddled him, she could feel his erection through his pants. The thought of his body—so sexy and large—moving inside her ignited a slow burn in her belly. She wanted him more now than when he'd first touched her.

She ran both hands over his abs, up his chest and out onto his well-defined biceps. And, hello, there were those shoulders. They were broad and ropy, making his torso taper into a manly vee that disappeared beneath the waistband of his jeans. Those jeans.

They were the only thing that still stood between them.

She inhaled sharply.

*Pace yourself.*

She steadied herself by allowing her hands to travel back down over his abs, memorizing his form and the feel of the muscles under her hands.

She was so caught up in the beauty and feel of him, of his skin on her skin, that she was a little startled when he rolled her over and his hands did the exploring. They glided over her hips, down to her thighs and dipped between them.

This was really going to happen. She was ready and hyperaware of every breath, every kiss, every touch. When his hand found her most vulnerable spot, she shivered with anticipation. She noticed that his body seemed to tremble, too.

She put a little space between them and slowly unzipped his jeans. Together they got him out of his pants and his underwear. Finally, when nothing stood between them, she reached out and brushed her fingertips over his manhood. His body shuddered. He inhaled a sharp breath and his body arched slightly. Even though she'd already gotten a good look at him, she devoured his male glory with her eyes, from his flat, muscled stomach…up farther to his biceps and his shoulders…to his throat and the chiseled planes of his face. She stroked him and learned every inch of him, committing his body to memory, but he didn't let her linger for long. He pulled away and picked up the condom packet, ripping it open. As she watched him put the condom on the generous length of his maleness, she thought she would go over the edge before they'd even began. Once everything was in place, he settled himself between her legs. She welcomed him by opening her thighs so that their bodies could join.

The physical sensations of what was happening made her shudder with excitement. He entered her with a tender, unhurried push. The heat that radiated from him seeped into her. His body was stiff as he gently inched forward, going so very slowly and being so careful. As her body adjusted to welcome him, she joined him in a slow rocking rhythm.

"Christopher," she whispered. "Oh… Christopher…"

Her sighs were lost in his kiss. He touched her with such care and seemed to instinctively know what her body wanted.

Pleasure began to rise and she angled her hips up to intensify the sensation. Their union seemed so very right that she cried out from the sheer pleasure of it.

She wanted him to feel good, too. She needed to touch him, to give him the same pleasure he was giving her. So she slid her hand between their bodies, reaching for him, wanting to heighten his pleasure. But he grabbed her wrist and held her hand firmly.

"Not yet," he said.

"Why?" she asked.

"Because. Just…not…yet." His breathlessness matched her own. "When you touch me, you make me…crazy. And this…this time is for you."

He stretched her arms up over her head and held them there as he rocked her toward her first release. As spasms of ecstasy overtook her body, his lips reclaimed hers.

The gentle, almost reverent way he touched her proved that he had been worth waiting for...but his hunger for her was never so evident as when he came up for air and devoured her with voracious eyes.

She couldn't get enough of his touch. As if he read her mind, he drove into her with such intensity she fisted her hands into the bed sheets and gasped, arching against him, propelled by the pulsing heat that was growing and throbbing inside her.

"Let yourself go," he said, his voice hoarse and husky. "Just let go, Kinsley."

Maybe it was the heat of his voice in her ear; more likely it was the way he made her body sing with his touch, but the next thing she knew he had driven her over the edge for the second time that night.

Again, he wrapped his arms around her, holding her tightly, protectively, until she had ridden out the wave.

She buried her face in his chest, breathing in the scent of him, of their joining, needing to get as close to him as possible. He continued to hold her tight. She lost herself again in his broad shoulders and the warmth of his strong arms.

"How was that?" His voice was a throaty rasp.

When she lifted her head and looked at him, his eyes searched her face.

"It was great. Really, breathtakingly great."

He smiled. "And I'm not finished yet."

The feel of his bare skin against hers almost put her into sensory overload.

She was so aware of him, of the two of them fused so closely that it seemed they were joined body and soul.

Christopher buried his head in the curve of her neck and let out a deep moan.

She eased her palms down his back, kissed him hard and fast and then things got a little crazy as she wrapped her legs around his waist and dug her nails into his shoulders. He didn't seem to mind how tightly she was clinging to him. So she held him in place by the shoulders and shifted under him. The way he groaned was so delicious that she arched beneath him again, drawing him deeper inside.

At that moment, staring down into her clear eyes, his body joined with hers, Christopher felt the mantle of his life shift. All of a sudden, without explanation, everything was different.

How could that happen now when it had never happened before?

Because he'd never been in love before now.

He was in love with Kinsley's laugh and her mind and the way she was able to set him straight without making him feel as if he'd been lambasted. He loved the way she felt in his arms right now, the smell of her smooth skin and the way she gazed up at him with a certain look in her eyes that was equal parts courage and vulnerability. It was everything he already knew about her and all the things he had yet to discover. He wanted to be the first face she saw in the morning and the last face she saw before she closed her eyes and drifted off to sleep at night. He wanted to be the shoulder she cried on and the lips she kissed.

He wanted to prove to her that all men weren't like her father, and she deserved someone who was crazy about her, someone who adored her the way she deserved to be loved.

He wanted to show her that love didn't have to hurt. The only problem was the prospect of doing that, rendering his heart that vulnerable, leaving it in someone else's hands, scared him to death.

But it was too late now. Judging by the way he felt, he had a feeling he'd already passed the point of no return.

"Christopher?" Kinsley's eyes searched his face. "Are you…okay?"

"I am absolutely better than okay." He kissed her deeply, pulling her to him so tightly that every inch of their bodies were merged. He hadn't particularly cared how close he'd felt to other women he'd been intimate with. But as he built up to the pace that would simultaneously transport Kinsley and him to nirvana, he wanted to see her face. He needed a one hundred percent connection. Not just body to body, but eye to eye and soul to soul.

It didn't take long before their bond, coupled with the rhythmic motion of their bodies, carried them over the edge together. As he lay with her, sweaty and spent, he cradled her against him.

As they'd made love, three words had been darting around inside his head. Now they'd somehow found their way to the tip of his tongue.

*Oh, man…. Don't do that,* he thought. *You're caught up in the moment. Don't say things you don't mean.*

The problem was, he did mean it. With all his soul.

Even so, meaning it and following through with the implications of *I love you* were two very different things.

Kinsley rolled over onto her stomach and looked up at him. "Are you really okay?"

He wanted to tell her exactly how he felt. Except when he opened his mouth all that came out was, "I've never been better."

Christopher wasn't used to being in this position of vulnerability. Since he'd been in Red Rock, he'd been used to being in command. But this woman lying in his arms had changed everything.

Frankly, it scared him to death.

## Chapter 12

Christopher didn't find his way home until late Sunday night. And that was only because he didn't have any suitable work clothes over at her place.

Once he was at home, with a little space to digest what had happened between them, he realized two very important things about himself: that he was in love with Kinsley, even if he didn't know how to tell her, and that he needed to be the one to reach out to his father and set their relationship on the road to right.

Funny, last week if someone had told him that falling in love would change him so much that he'd be willing to extend the olive branch to Deke, he would've told them to go to hell.

But here he was, at nine o'clock on Sunday night, staring at his cell phone as he dialed his parents' number.

He had to do it now before he changed his mind or the spell that Kinsley had cast on him wore off.

Somehow, he didn't believe that this call would do any good. His old man was as stubborn as a bulldog that had clamped down on a stick. Once Deke sank his teeth into something there was no prying it loose. Everything in his world was black-and-white. He wasn't about to change his mind about his son.

How his sweet mother had put up with him all these years was a mystery. As he listened to the phone ring two-three-four times, the realization washed over Christopher that the reason he had decided to be the one to reach out and try to make amends was so he could know in his heart that he had done everything in his power to not be like his father.

Good, bad or indifferent, it had taken him a while to realize that. And it had taken the childhood experiences of a great woman to help him reframe his situation and see his family with a new appreciation. Kinsley was right, the family you took for granted wasn't going to be there forever. Having lost both of her parents within a one-year period, Kinsley was living proof of this.

Her father sounded like a monster. While Deke could be difficult, the old coot had never emotionally or physically abused his family. Sure he was hard on them. You could say a lot of things about Deke Jones, but he always did right by his family. Or at least, his version of right.

Wasn't that something to hold on to? Something to focus on? Because when he put it all into perspective, Christopher knew his upbringing could've been a whole lot worse.

It was probably too late to call the house on a Sunday night, anyway. Deke, the creature of habit he was, had probably been in bed for a good half hour.

Maybe, subconsciously, he'd known that and that was the reason he'd decided to call…or maybe he shouldn't overthink it. He could try again tomorrow.

Christopher had just pulled the phone away from his ear, when he heard a craggy voice grunt and gruff, "Hello?"

Hesitating, Christopher drew in a breath as he brought the phone to his ear.

"Hello?" the man repeated, the irritation in his voice mounting.

Deke and Jeanne Marie didn't have caller ID so there was no way he would've known it was his son. In his mind's eye Christopher could see Deke giving the phone a dirty look before he slammed the receiver back into the cradle.

"Pops? It's Chris."

Silence answered him. For a moment he wondered if Deke had already hung up. But then the old man said, "Son?" His voice was so soft, it was barely audible and most un-Deke-like.

"Yeah, Pops, it's me. Is this a good time? I hope I'm not calling too late."

Christopher waited for Deke to cut him off at the knees as he was so fond of doing. The old man had had two months to stew on his anger at Chris for abandoning the ranch to take a desk job pushing papers, for disassociating himself from the Jones name, moving to Red Rock and surely a plethora of other sins real or imagined of which he had found Christopher guilty.

"You can ring this house at midnight and I would take your call, son. It's good to hear your voice."

As Deke's positive response registered,

Christopher exhaled a breath he didn't realize he'd been holding. On the other end of the line, he heard his father call to his mom. "Jeanne, it's Chris on the phone. Get in here."

"Chris, it's ladies first. Talk to your mama and then she'll give me the phone."

His mother was her usual, sweet, unconditional self, saying how much she and the family had missed him but that they all understood that he was making a nice life for himself in Red Rock.

"I do wish you would come home to visit soon," she said, her voice a little wistful. "You don't know what I'd give to hug you."

Christopher made noises about being busy at work but promised that he would see what he could do about arranging some time off for a visit. He thought about telling her that she and Deke were always welcome in Red Rock but decided against it. Deke would never hear of making the trip. Not even if it was his wife's dying wish— Christopher stopped himself from tumbling down the path of negativity that he usually traveled when he conversed with his father. Old Deke had started the conversation off nicely enough. Even though it raised his hackles, Christopher forced himself to take the high road and not instigate an argument…and to refuse the invitation if Deke invited him to one.

"I got the photo album you made for me, Mama. I really appreciate it."

"I wanted you to have some pictures from Toby and Angie's wedding. We all missed you. It was a beautiful day, but it would've been even better if you had stood up with your brother."

A pang of guilt stabbed Christopher right in the heart. He grabbed the album off the end table where it had been hidden under a stack of magazines and financial newspapers since he'd brought it home from the office.

He opened it to a page featuring a five-by-seven photo of the smiling bride and groom. He flipped the page and saw another of the entire family—minus him, of course—gathered around his brother and his new sister-in-law.

It really had been ridiculous and selfish to miss such an important occasion. But with the frame of mind he'd been in then and as mad as Deke had been at him, there was no way he was going to cast a dark shadow over his brother's big day.

He heard Kinsley's voice in the back of his head saying, *Don't dwell on things you can't change. Look forward and spend that energy on things that matter.*

Toby understood why he'd stayed away and that was all that mattered. Still, a funny feeling circled in his gut like a shark poised to attack.

"It was great to see Toby when he and Angie were here in town. Will you please be sure and tell him I called?"

"I sure will, honey. But I'm going to hand the phone over to your dad now. He's getting a little antsy waiting to talk to you."

*Right.* That would be the day the sky fell when Deke stood antsy with anticipation waiting to talk to his black-sheep son. Christopher wanted to snort, but he didn't. Instead, he told his mother he loved her and promised her one more time that he would do his best to make it home for a visit as soon as he could manage.

Then he put on his emotional armor and prepared for Deke to shoot him like a sniper poised and ready high atop a building.

"Well, now it's my turn," Deke said.

Christopher held his tongue, unsure if that was sarcasm or sincerity in his dad's tone.

"You made your mama really happy by calling tonight, son."

Oh. Okay. Could it have been sincerity? Or was it a verbal trap designed to lure Christopher into a false sense of security so that Deke could turn around and sucker punch?

He closed the photo album and set it on the coffee table, scooting forward so that he was sitting on the edge of the couch.

"It was good to hear her voice," Christopher said. In a split second he decided to stick to his original plan and play nice. "It's good to hear yours, too, Pops."

The words hung out there for a few beats before Deke answered, "I'm glad to talk to you, too. Son, I have a confession to make. I regret the way we parted when you took off for Red Rock. You and I have had our differences over the years, but we've never left things so badly between us."

The old Christopher would have quipped, "You regretted it so much that you waited for me to call so you could tell me." But from his view on the high road, he could see that this was a hard confession for Deke to make.

"I've regretted it, too, Pops. I'm… I'm sorry."

As soon as the words escaped Christopher clamped his mouth shut, gritting his teeth so hard he could feel it all the way up to his temples.

"That's right big of you to say that, boy. To be the first one to apologize." Deke's voice sounded small and…humble? So much so that Christopher wasn't even sure it really was his father on the other end of the line.

"How's that job of yours going?" Deke asked.

So in the end his father couldn't bring himself to say the two little words that would have gone such a long way toward healing them… reuniting their family. Then again, maybe this was Deke's version of an apology. Christopher swallowed his pride and decided it was.

"It's great. I'm really enjoying it. Working for the Foundation is giving me a lot of opportunities to do some good in the community."

And that was as far as he was going to justify what he did for a living.

"That's what I hear. James has been in touch with your mama and he's had a lot of good things to say about you. He bragged about you, saying that you have a great work ethic and a real creative head for business. He says you've been such an asset to the Foundation, he would've hired you even if you weren't a blood relative. I'm really proud of you, son."

*Proud of you, son.*

Christopher fell back against the couch cushions so hard it knocked some of the air out of his lungs in a *whoosh*.

For the first time in his life, his father had told him he was *proud* of him. Christopher had a hard time hearing the rest of what his father said because of the blood rushing in his ears.

Family could be the most amazing people in your life while simultaneously being the most exasperating.

If an apology was gold, the words that had just passed from Deke's lips and traveled four hundred miles through the phone line were platinum.

No, they were priceless.

What was the Foundation's policy about fraternizing with a superior?

As Kinsley flipped through the employee handbook, she silently chastised herself. *Now was a heck of a time to worry about that.*

Still, for her own peace of mind she needed to know. After Christopher left her on Sunday evening, Kinsley had fallen back to earth with a terrifying awareness of her vulnerability.

She'd decided when she saw Christopher again, it should be business as usual. If they were going to work together, they had to keep their emotions (and libidos) in check.

Or at least *she* had to.

That sounded like common sense, but it was

easier said than done. Now she was having a hard time keeping her mind on work when she knew Christopher was right across the hall.

That was the problem. He sat right. Across. The hall. And that's where he'd been, holed up in his office, for the better part of the day Monday.

Now it was midday Tuesday and he hadn't come into the office yet, which was no big deal. Before things had *changed* between them, she hadn't felt it necessary to know his schedule. They had never checked in with each other. Why should they do that now? It was a ridiculous thought.

Yet every time she heard a deep voice in the reception area she looked up, hoping to catch a glimpse of him.

To no avail.

He was acting as if nothing had happened between them. He wasn't exactly avoiding her. Or maybe he was…she wouldn't know because she hadn't seen him except for late yesterday afternoon, when she'd run into him as she was on her way out and he was on his way in. He'd held the elevator door for her, and he had acted like the same old Christopher—the "before sex" Christopher. After the initial exchange of hi-how-are-yous, he'd mentioned that he had the germ of a wonderful idea for educating people on how to intervene when they saw someone being bullied. He had been saddened and inspired by what had happened to Tonya at the Spring Fling.

"Maybe we can talk about it soon?"

"Absolutely," she'd said, trying to figure out if he had run with the idea because he knew how important the cause was to her. Then again, adding another leg to the bullying prevention campaign would reflect well on him, too.

Although she hadn't expected him to kiss her at the elevator, she had wished for a little more. A whispered *Saturday night rocked my world;* a *Let's do it again soon;* or even better, *What are you doing for dinner tonight?*

He looked as if he was about to say something, but the elevator had buzzed, scolding them for holding the doors open too long.

He'd simply said, "Don't let me keep you," and she'd answered, "Good night," and had gotten into the elevator...alone with her pride.

She wasn't about to let herself appear needy because at that point, weren't his feelings pretty clear?

Today, after paging through the handbook no fewer than five times, she still couldn't find the answer to her question about superior/subordinate relationships. Did that mean there was no policy? And why wasn't there one? Probably because not sleeping with your superior/subordinate was common sense—something every savvy professional knew.

Instead of driving herself crazy dwelling on it, she busied herself doing something more productive: polishing the recap of the Spring Fling event for the staff meeting next week.

As she was reading through her draft, her mind drifted. Maybe she should call him and ask him where they stood?

And maybe she should just stamp the word NEEDY on her forehead.

*Stop it.*

She had two choices. She could talk to Christopher about it, or be confident that things would turn out the way they were meant to be.

She had always prided herself on being confident. She had never obsessed over things she couldn't control, and she wasn't going to start now.

Realizing that her eyes had been scanning the recap but her mind had been thinking about Christopher and nothing of what she had just read had registered, she started back at the top of the page and forced herself to focus.

Bev buzzed her phone.

"Hey, Kinsley," she said. "Sawyer Fortune is on line one for you."

*Sawyer Fortune?*

"Thank you, Bev."

She pressed Line One.

"This is Kinsley Aaron."

"Hi, Kinsley, it's Sawyer Fortune. Am I catching you at a good time?"

"Absolutely, Sawyer," she said. "How can I help you?"

"I've been trying to reach Christopher today, but he seems to be unavailable. When I met with him the last time I was in town, he mentioned that the two of you worked closely in the community relations department, so I thought I would run it by you."

Sawyer went on to tell her about possible dates for the air-show fund-raiser that would benefit the Foundation. She assured him that she would talk to Christopher today and make sure he got back with Sawyer as soon as possible to reserve the date.

*So, Christopher had even been unavailable to Sawyer.*

That shed a new light on things. Something was up. Maybe that meant he wasn't avoiding her.

She was about to hang up with Sawyer when he said, "Oh, and, Kinsley, thanks for talking Christopher into calling his father. When I last spoke to Christopher, he said he had talked to Deke and that you were the one who had urged him to do so."

A knot of emotions formed in Kinsley's stomach as she mumbled something to Sawyer, then hung up the phone. He had called his father. That was great, a true breakthrough for him. He had told Sawyer that he had done so at her urging. That was tremendous, especially because he had mentioned her to Sawyer yesterday. She could let her mind go in all sorts of directions, imagining what he had said about her to his cousin.

But why did there always have to be a qualifier? If she had been the one who convinced him to take such an important step, why hadn't he shared the news with her? It was pretty important. He could've said something when they were standing at the elevator.

A cold, prickling realization settled around Kinsley. Maybe he hadn't shared this personal news with her because it was *personal*.

Maybe she needed to take a hint from his lack of communication over the past day and a half.

A bubble of laughter escaped, but the sound was dry and devoid of humor. Despite Christopher's claims to the contrary, he had a love-'em-and-leave-'em reputation. Facts were facts. She had put too much stock into their night together. Their...liaison.

Oh, God. That was all it had been.

Icy hot humiliation settled around her. She bit her lip until it throbbed in time with her pulse. She sat there—just sat there—for several long minutes, letting reality seep into her pores, flogging herself with I-told-you-sos.

*You knew this was a very plausible outcome.* Whenever she violated her gut instinct, she always lived to regret it.

Now, if she knew what was good for her, she'd get herself together. No moping. No sniping at Christopher. No looking back with regret.

She would not let this interfere with her work.

Because in her work, she would find the solidity that would distract her and camouflage the despair that colored everything in sight.

For what must've been the hundredth time, Kinsley reminded herself that the Fortunes considered blood thicker than water. She didn't want to chance losing her job should someone disapprove of her affair with Christopher. Or worse yet, if talk started around the office that Kinsley was attempting to sleep her way to the top, Christopher might see her as a burden and decide the office would be better off without her.

If she had learned one thing growing up in an abusive home, it was that the less attention you drew to yourself, the better off—the safer—you were in the long run. That meant no more jealous outbursts like the time she thought he was dating his etiquette coach.

From this moment forward, she would put a smile on her face and it would be business as usual.

Good thing, too, because when she looked up, Christopher was standing in her doorway smiling and holding a big presentation board.

Christopher was simply flat-out scared to fall in love. He recognized that but had no idea what to do, besides stop hiding and acting like a child. Kinsley deserved better than that.

He knew he had been distant, using the excuse that he had been immersed in work, busy coming up with a plan for them to use as a follow-up to the initiative that they'd started at the Spring Fling.

But if he were completely honest with himself, he had been avoiding Kinsley. By doing so, he didn't have to face his feelings.

Why could he analyze so easily, but he had no idea what to do with it?

He had been heartened by his father's newfound respect and bolstered by his uncle's good report.

With this newfound support system, in a day and a half he had managed to outline the basics of the follow-up program. His initial reaction had him wanting to involve Kinsley, but fear caused him to back away. He simply needed a cooling-off period, time to put things into perspective and remember how to be her colleague without wanting to undress her and lay her flat across his desk.

But seeing her at the elevator yesterday, he knew that his silence was hurting her. Hell, it was hurting *him*. But last night he'd decided that in a similar way that he'd reached out to Deke, he needed to break the ice with Kinsley.

He thought the best way to do that—at least, for starters—was to ask her opinion on the new idea.

As he stood in her office doorway, gripping the presentation board, he felt the same pull of attraction that he felt every time he looked at her.

"May I come in?" he asked.

Her blue eyes looked wary as she smiled at him. Her professional smile. He recognized it.

"Sure," she said.

He left the door open on purpose, to discourage the conversation from veering off on a personal path.

"Remember how I told you yesterday that I had come up with a new plan for us to use in the schools?"

She nodded. Yep. Her wall was up. He recognized that, too.

"This is intended as a tool for school guidance counselors to use." Damn, this was harder than he had expected. The way she was looking at him…it was more like she was staring right through him. "I hope that it will help kids remember to not just stand there when someone is in trouble, but to act."

He realized that he was nervous as he turned the board around, showing her the acronym GET INVOLVED. Each letter of the words stood for an element of the program.

Christopher watched Kinsley as she read the board, her lips pressed into a thin line.

When she was finished, she simply nodded

and said, "Get Involved, huh? That's good advice. Even if it is a little ironic coming from a man who seems to do everything in his power to avoid doing exactly that."

## *Chapter 13*

On Wednesday morning, Christopher still couldn't get Kinsley's face out of his head. The way she'd looked as she'd read the GET INVOLVED acronym.

She'd had good reason for looking so upset. The words obviously hit home.

Sitting at his desk, he rested his forehead on his palm. He was such an idiot. How could he not have seen the irony of the message before he brought it to her?

As soon as she'd read it, he'd seen it in her eyes. Sure, she kept a professional poker face, but she couldn't disguise the hurt. She'd told him it was perfect and then excused herself, saying she had a lunch engagement.

She'd walked out, leaving him sitting there with his presentation board on the desk and his foot in his mouth. He needed to practice what he preached.

GET INVOLVED?

His problem was that he was too afraid to get involved. So ridiculously terrified—of what? He had better figure it out because his fear was going to cost him the best thing that had ever happened to him.

They needed to talk about this. Even if he didn't know what to say. He needed to let her know it wasn't her; it was him. That she was smart and beautiful and deserving of so much more than he could offer.

He picked up the phone to call her office. But then he put it back down in the cradle. Maybe he should just go talk to her. Common sense told him he should wait until after work. He didn't want to upset her, but that seemed as though he wasn't giving her enough credit.

He got up from his desk and made his way into the reception area, but before he could get to Kinsley's office, Bev intercepted him.

"Mr. Jamison just called," she said. "He wants to see you in his office right away."

Christopher made his way to Emmett Jamison's wing of the building. His administrative assistant, Clara, was expecting him.

"Oh, good, there you are," she said. "He wants to see you but he has another meeting at 10:30." She glanced at her watch. "Oh, no problem. You have plenty of time. Go right in."

As Christopher walked toward Emmett's door, he heard Clara inform him that Christopher was on his way in.

For a fleeting second, he wondered if this had to do with the talk he had had with his father. But then that gave way to the guilt he felt over how things had turned out with Kinsley. Surely, she wouldn't have lodged a complaint against him, would she?

No, that would be completely out of character for her. But he couldn't ignore the little voice that jabbed at him and said she would be completely within her rights. He should've been stronger and not taken advantage of her while she was vulnerable, even though that's not at all what he had intended.

The same jabbing voice brought up words like love and feelings, but he ignored it as he rapped on Emmett's door.

"Come in."

Christopher opened the door and stepped

inside. He was immediately set at ease by the broad smile that graced Emmett's face.

"Just the man I wanted to see," Emmett said. "Have a seat, please." He gestured to a chair in front of his desk.

Christopher complied.

As soon as he was settled Emmett picked up the display board that outlined the GET INVOLVED program. He tapped it with his finger.

"This is good work."

He paused, as if letting the praise ring in the air.

"You have done some impressive work in your short time here at the Foundation. I'm not the only one who has taken notice. But before I tell you what I have in mind, let me ask you, are you happy with what you're doing? Because you sure are doing a good job."

"I love what I'm doing. I truly feel like I've found my calling here at the Foundation."

"Great, that's exactly what I was hoping you would say. I have an opportunity I would like to talk to you about. We have discovered the need for a presence in New York City. I know New York is very different than Red Rock, but the work would be similar. We—the board, your uncle James, Lily and I—were hoping that you would be willing to take on the challenge. How would you feel about relocating to New York City and opening that office for us? We would love for you to be the man in charge. If anyone can do it, you could."

Emmett's offer caught Christopher so off guard, he couldn't even answer for a moment. He was truly stunned.

New York City? They wanted him to move out there and open the office?

*But what about Kinsley?*

"Would anyone else be in the office with me?" he asked. "Would I have a staff?"

Emmett steepled his fingers. "Not right off the bat. We would have to make sure that the new office was up and running and self-sustaining, of course—there's no mission without margin—before we could fully staff the office. But don't worry. We would pay to relocate you and give you a salary increase and housing allowance that would allow you to live comfortably in the city."

Of course, it would mean leaving behind everybody he had come to care so much about.

Kinsley's face was the first to flash in his mind again. Even before his newfound relatives and all the friends he had made since moving to Red Rock.

It was a tempting offer. It meant that they trusted him. It meant that they respected him and appreciated his vision. Uncle James, Lily and Emmett were the first people who had truly believed in him.

That inappropriate voice piped up inside him and reminded him that Kinsley had once believed in him too.

"I realize that this is a lot to think about," said Emmett. "I will have Clara draw up the specifics and get them to you by the end of the day. Why don't you take a few days to think about it before you let me know your answer? The sooner we can get you there, the better."

Christopher cleared his throat. "I want you to know how much I appreciate your confidence in me. I am greatly honored and humbled that you would entrust me with this position. I'll look forward to reviewing the details."

Emmett stood and offered Christopher his hand. Christopher stood and accepted it. What would Deke and Jeanne Marie think of this? His father had had a conniption when Christopher had accepted the job in Red Rock. If his father had thought this place was highfalutin, what in the world would he think of his son moving to New York City?

But Christopher reminded himself not to get

too far ahead. He hadn't seen the offer yet. He had no idea what they intended in terms of dollars and cents.

Even though he wasn't anywhere close to making up his mind, he knew one of the biggest sacrifices he would be making would be leaving Kinsley behind.

Suddenly everything that had been so muddled and tentative seemed to snap into sharp focus. This job was everything he had ever wanted, except it didn't include Kinsley. But maybe time away from her in a place where he could focus on his job and not be distracted by her full lips and the way their bodies fit so perfectly together that it drove him nuts to even catch a glimpse of her in the office hallway was a good thing.

Maybe putting some distance between them was exactly what he needed. Then again, maybe this opportunity would cost him the one woman he had ever loved. But maybe that was case in point why he should go and not look back.

That evening Christopher sat at his desk reading—for the fifth time—the details of the generous New York City relocation offer that Clara had delivered to him just before five o'clock.

Among other perks, they were offering him nearly twice his current salary and a housing allowance that would afford him a comfortable apartment in Manhattan.

It was a far cry from Horseback Hollow and the life sentence on his family's ranch. This offer was a dream come true. And more than that, it was validation that he was good at his job. The board could've chosen anyone to head up this project, but they'd put their faith in him.

Christopher closed the file and leaned back in his leather chair, stretching his feet out in front of him and looking around his office. When he'd first gotten here, he'd thought this place was the be-all and end-all with its paneled walls, living room furniture and that view.

Now, he'd been handed the chance of a lifetime to write his own ticket.

So why was he hesitating?

The numbers checked out. It would be a long time before a chance like this would come along again, much less be dropped into his lap.

He needed to think about it. Sleep on it. Even if Emmett was pushing for a fast answer, Christopher needed a few hours to process everything. Then maybe this uncertainty would sort itself out.

In his head it was a no-brainer: only idiots passed up the chance of a lifetime for a woman. Especially when he'd had trepidations about their relationship before the deal was on the table.

However, now that the deal was on the table, his head and his heart were at odds.

He'd have to sort that out, and fast.

He put the file in his briefcase and clicked off his desk lamp.

It was after 6:30 p.m. The sun was painting the Western landscape outside his window in shades of gold and amber. Everything looked a little different in the light of this offer. As Christopher headed toward the elevator, the light that was still on in Kinsley's office drew him like a moth.

She was completely engaged in whatever it was she was reading on her computer screen. He stood there watching her, wanting to memorize the way she looked right now with her guard down and her hair hanging in soft curls around her shoulders. He owed it to her to tell her about the offer before she heard it from someone else.

"Don't you ever go home?" he said.

She startled and looked up at him. "Oh, Christopher. I didn't realize anyone else was still here."

"Just you and me," he said, his heart compressing at the words. "Do you have a minute?"

She pushed her mouse away and angled her body toward him. "Sure, come in."

He settled himself in the chair across from her.

"Everything okay?" she asked. Her hand fluttered to her blouse collar and she fidgeted with the top button, which, as always, was buttoned up tight.

Despite everything, he had to resist the urge to reach out and undo it and all the others and pull her into him so that he could lose himself in the Nirvana that was her.

And that was exactly why he needed to distance himself. He couldn't even think straight when he was with her. It was his own fault. Yep, it was all on him, and he needed to do something to regain his equilibrium.

"Everything is fine. More than fine, actually. I got a job offer today."

Her expression remained neutral. "Really? Where?"

"New York."

He told her how Emmett had called him into his office earlier.

"It's great money, and such an opportunity I can't see how I can refuse."

For a split second he thought he saw a flicker of regret flash in her blue eyes, and in that same split second he knew that if she said, "Don't go," he wouldn't. He'd turn down the offer and he'd take her home and make love to her until they'd finally figured out that this complicated thing between them didn't have to be so—

"How wonderful for you," she said, verbally slapping the sense back into him. "When do you leave for New York?"

Kinsley was happy for Christopher. Truly, she was.

And she had told him that yesterday when he stopped by her office. She said it with her most genuine smile.

She wanted him to be happy.

Really, she did. And if she kept telling herself how happy she was that he was leaving, maybe she would start to believe it.

Even though she hadn't seen the specifics of the offer yet, Kinsley knew he would take it. The Fortunes were generous with their compensation. There was no way he would turn it down.

His leaving was probably the very best thing that could happen to both of them. He would relocate to a place where he could steep himself in big city, sophistication. She could keep her job here and maybe regain her concentration…and her heart.

Of course it would end up this way. Of course it would. This proved that it really was best that they hadn't committed to each other.

It was hard enough to know that he didn't want a relationship with her. The only thing that might've been harder was knowing that he did want a relationship and then him having to choose between her and his dream job.

She laughed to herself as she realized she had gotten it wrong. Women weren't Christopher's mistress; his work was.

She sat there trying to convince herself that this really was the best thing for both of them. If she said the words enough, surely she would begin to believe it. If not now, maybe by the time he made the move. Just then an email popped up in her computer inbox. Kinsley sat up a little straighter when she realized it was from Lily Cassidy Fortune.

The subject line read Surprise party for Christopher.

Kinsley clicked on the email.

Hello, Kinsley, I am calling on you for a rather large favor. Since you seem to be the colleague closest to Christopher, would you please take on the task of organizing a surprise going-away party for him? I was hoping we could do something nice for him—something a touch sentimental? I will leave it in your capable hands as I'm sure you will know exactly what to do to make Christopher realize how much he means to us and how grateful we are that he has accepted this challenge. We were hoping to have the party tomorrow, as he will be making the move this weekend. I know this is all terribly fast, but I'm sure Beverly will be happy to assist you with anything you need.

Kinsley fell back against her chair and her breath rushed from her lungs.

*So it was official.*

And he was leaving this weekend?

Christopher was leaving *this* weekend?

Her heart cracked open and filled with a leaden dread.

She wasn't surprised that he had accepted

it. He'd all but made up his mind when they'd talked last night. She just hadn't realized he would leave so soon.

She fought the sudden urge to cry, blinking back the unwelcome tears that clouded her vision. There was no use getting emotional. It was for the best.

Really, it was.

She needed to treat this the same way one would rip off a bandage—the faster the better. The sooner Christopher got on with his new life, the sooner she could get on with her life here in Red Rock without him.

She sat there for several minutes in her quiet office, listening to the whirr of the air conditioner and the hum of her computer. Now that the tears were at bay, a strange numbness had overtaken her.

She picked up the phone and called Bev.

They had less than twenty-four hours. They would have to get this party planning rolling as soon as possible if they were going to pull it off.

The sooner they started planning, the sooner it would be over.

## Chapter 14

*"SURPRISE!"*

The chorus of voices rang out when Emmett opened the conference room door and ushered Christopher inside.

Christopher blinked once, twice, three times as he looked around at all of his coworkers who had crowded into the conference room, surrounded by streamers and helium balloons.

"What the heck is this?"

His uncle James stepped forward and clapped him on the back. "This is your party, son. We wanted to give you a good sendoff on your last day here in the Red Rock office."

*A surprise party?*

He glanced at Emmett and murmured something unintelligible. Emmett grinned back at him, obviously proud that his paper-signing ruse had worked to get him to the conference room.

Christopher *was* surprised. Surprised and genuinely touched that everyone would gather on a Friday afternoon—just for him.

There were steaming covered chafing dishes in the middle of the conference room table being tended to by catering staff in uniforms with the Red logo. His stomach growled as he inhaled the delicious aroma of Red's Mexican food—a mélange of savory dishes blending with the aroma of fresh corn tortillas, chilies and spices. There were platters of Red's famous corn roasted in the husk stacked on platters which were next to the biggest cake he had ever seen in his life. And there was champagne.

That's when he realized that everyone was raising a glass toward him. Lily stepped forward and handed him and Emmett each a flute, too.

Emmett and James, who were flanking Christopher, simultaneously touched their glasses to his.

"I would like to propose a toast," said James.

"To Christopher Fortune, our golden boy. May you shine in the city as brightly as you do here."

"To Christopher!" someone shouted and everyone raised their glasses a little higher, then took a sip.

Christopher glanced around the room, taking in his family, friends and coworkers: Miguel and Marcos Mendoza were there. So was their cousin Sierra Mendoza Calloway. Standing next to her was Emmett's wife, Linda Faraday. She was talking to Susan Fortune Eldridge and Julie Osterman Fortune. Nicholas and Jeremy Fortune were there. Then he saw Tanner and Jordana Redmond and Sawyer and his wife, Laurel—had they come all the way from Horseback Hollow to be here just for him?

As people surrounded him, offering handshakes, high fives and fist bumps, he realized how much he truly cared for these people.

It was a bit overwhelming.

Funny, before he got here, when he had first taken on the Fortune name, he had imagined them all to be so different than they had turned out to be. Not in a bad way. In fact, they were better than he could've ever imagined. They were all warm, loving, family-oriented people, and he was proud to be one of them.

And when Sawyer came over and shook his hand, Christopher experienced an inexplicable pang of homesickness for his immediate family in Horseback Hollow. Even Deke.

Especially Deke.

As the good wishes continued and people rallied around him—it was a good thing he wasn't claustrophobic—he found himself craning his neck searching for the one person he was desperate to see.

Finally, he saw Kinsley standing by the table with the champagne, refilling glasses, doing what she was so good at—helping other people.

His gaze was drawn to her like a pin to a magnet. He drank her in, trying to take a mental snapshot of her gorgeous face, her blue-blue eyes that were framed by eyebrows a few shades darker than her sun-streaked blond hair. Her finely chiseled cheekbones. The delicate slope of her neck. Her full lips.

He could still feel those lips on his. He could feel the way their bodies had fit so perfectly, as if they were made for each other. A surge of longing so deep and fraught with desire for her consumed him.

It was as if he were seeing her for the first time. Through new eyes. Now he wanted her even more than he had the first time he'd seen her.

Why was it that he never really appreciated what he had when he had it? Why did he always wonder if something better was around the corner? Standing here in the midst of the crowd, among all these well-wishers, his heart spoke loud and clear: there wasn't a better woman in the world for him than Kinsley Aaron.

He had to tamp down the urge to fight his way through the crowd and pull her into his arms. His heart ached for her.

As much as he loved the attention and the accolades and the thought that his uncle James and Lily Cassidy Fortune trusted him—*him,* the guy who never seemed to have the capability to do anything right back in Horseback Hollow—with opening their satellite office in a city like New York, and even though they had been more than generous with the compensation and benefits package that they had given him, moving to New York would mean losing touch with everyone that mattered to him.

And it would mean losing Kinsley.

Suddenly his future flashed before his eyes in a crystal-clear vision: he would have the money and the dream job and the prestige and everything he could ever want at his disposal in a big city where the world would be his oyster, but it would never be enough. He would never be satisfied with all of that because it was empty. Well, the work had proved to be fulfilling, but all the money in the world couldn't replace what he had found in Red Rock.

Being here, he had learned how to go home again.

He had learned the value of everything money couldn't buy.

Was he really willing to give up everything for...emptiness?

He excused himself from his colleagues and made his way over to Emmett and James, who were standing with Linda and Lily.

"This is a fabulous party," Christopher said. "I can't thank you enough."

Lily set a slender hand on his arm. "Oh, honey, I wish we could all take credit for this party. But this is all Kinsley Aaron. Is there anything that woman can't do? Didn't she do a lovely job?"

"There is absolutely nothing she can't do," Christopher said. "She's even taught me a thing or two since I've been working with her. So I'm not at all surprised to learn that she is the one responsible for this."

Christopher watched Kinsley as she cut the cake and put small squares on the colorful party plates. He watched her as she worked while everyone else was enjoying themselves. She was always willing to go the extra mile for somebody else. Always willing to sacrifice even if it meant standing back while somebody else shined.

How could he have been such a damn fool?

How could he have been willing to let go of the only woman in this world he would ever be able to love?

Christopher turned to James and Emmett. "If you don't mind, I need to speak to the two of you privately."

Both men did a double-take.

"Right now?" asked James. "In case you didn't notice, son, there's a party going on. Rumor has it it's in your honor."

"That's exactly why I need to talk to you now," said Christopher. "This can't wait."

*Just keep yourself busy and it'll be over faster.*

Kinsley was not in the mood to party. But

she sure was good at playing the role of the hostess.

She reminded herself that this was not about her. It had nothing to do with her. She needed to keep smiling and keep her eye on the light at the end of the tunnel.

It would all be over soon.

So, Kinsley refilled the tortilla platters and the water pitchers. She brought out extra bottles of soda and champagne and replenished the paper goods, cups and the plastic utensils.

As she looked around, she caught a glimpse of Christopher. He was talking to Mr. Jamison, Lily Fortune and James Marshall Fortune. She looked away but not before she felt the heat of his gaze on her.

But then, when she glanced back, he was gone. Probably hidden by one of the one hundred balloons in the room. She breathed a sigh of relief and moved around the chafing dishes the catering staff had just replenished.

Good grief, these people were tough customers. From the way they were devouring the food you would think they hadn't eaten in days. But who could blame them? Red prided itself on delicious food. Today they offered beef brisket enchiladas, chicken mole and spicy lobster tacos. She was having to hustle now, but the more they ate, the less she and the staff would have to clean up later.

And the more work she would have to keep her hands busy and her mind off the reason for the party.

*Christopher.* The mere thought of him made her chest tighten and her heart squeeze.

*Stop it.*

But what good did fighting it do? She kept her head down and allowed herself to switch over to autopilot. To let the thoughts and feelings come and go as they would. Maybe if she leaned into the emotions she'd have an easier time of it.

Or maybe she would break down into a heaping, sobbing mess and really humiliate herself. She took a deep breath and released it slowly.

No, it seemed that the thoughts and feelings were hidden deep enough under the surface. Even so, everyone else in this room was so convivial and having such a good time that no one had a clue that her heart was breaking.

Scratch that. Her heart had already broken. Past tense. For days, she had been carrying around a bunch of bits and pieces of broken heart that she knew would never be able to fit back together again.

That was okay. She didn't have any use for her heart anymore. She just hoped the pieces didn't rattle.

Stepping outside of herself, she had to admit that Christopher had seemed astonished. It was always nice when a surprise party went off the way it was planned.

*That's right. Focus on the good. There you go.*

She resisted the urge to look up and search the crowd for him. So far, playing caterer had helped her to not moon over him, to not watch what he was doing or who he was talking to. It just hurt too much.

Plus, the last thing she needed was for someone she worked with to discover her secret: that she was brokenhearted because had slept with Christopher and the affair had gone horribly, disastrously wrong. *That* could be misconstrued in so many ways.

Normally, she didn't care what people thought of her. But this was a different case. She may have lost her heart, but it was imperative for her to walk away with her integrity and dignity intact. Because what had happened between Christopher and her hadn't been like that. She wasn't using him to get favors or a boost up the corporate ladder.

It was…

Yeah, it was.

And it was over now. She needed to get over it. But it had only been a week since she had given herself—body and soul—to him; her heart still felt tender and her pride was pretty raw.

What had she expected? She knew what she had wanted. But what you want and what you get were sometimes two entirely different things.

What she had gotten was a lesson. She didn't give her heart away easily. And she wouldn't do it again anytime soon. After all, who would want the bag of broken pieces she stored in the place where her heart had once lived?

She would feel better someday. It would just take time. Right now she needed to keep her chin up.

*Chin up, buttercup.* Her mom used to say that when they'd hit a rough patch. God, what she wouldn't give to be able to go to her mother right now. Not for advice, but for a shoulder. For the shelter of her hugs. She had been the one person in whom Kinsley had found unrequited love.

And if she'd learned one thing from watching her mother it was that sometimes when you loved too much your generous spirit became your undoing.

Unlike her mother, she had a second chance to reclaim herself. Rather than mooning, she would embrace the blessing in this narrow miss.

*Right*...

Forcing herself to look up, she glanced around the room admiring her handiwork—not looking for Christopher. Everyone was chatting, and the buzz of convivial energy filled the room. The helium balloons she had procured did a fairly decent job of hiding her—or hiding him. Either way, because they were clustered in the area where she had been hiding out, she had to make an effort to look for him. As if blatantly defying her, her eyes swept the room looking for him, but before she could pick him out she came face-to-face with a giant yellow balloon...well, what better caution sign could a girl ask for?

She was running the risk of driving herself crazy, so she made another conscious effort to refocus. She scanned the food tables in search of something to distract her, but it appeared that everyone was finally slowing down. Nothing needed refilling or replenishing or replacing.

She picked up a couple of empty cups and plates, realizing if she felt like the hired help, it was because she had put herself in that position. The catering staff would take care of this. She swiped the back of her hand across her forehead, then tucked an errant strand of hair behind her ear.

Maybe she would have a glass of champagne. She didn't really feel like celebrating, but that was no reason to boycott the bubbly. In fact, looking on the bright side, she should celebrate the fact that she'd pulled this off.

Who would've thought that planning a party would be one of the hardest assignments she'd ever faced?

The old adage what doesn't kill you makes you stronger definitely applied here.

She had just poured herself a glass of champagne when Mr. Jamison called everyone in the conference room to order.

"May I have your attention, please? Everyone, please settle down and listen. Christopher has something he would like to say."

*Oh, boy. Here we go.*

The room quieted down and everybody turned their attention to Christopher. For the first time that afternoon, Kinsley stopped what she was doing and gave him her ears.

Mr. Jamison turned to Christopher and murmured, "Are you sure this is what you want to do?"

Christopher nodded. "Actually, I've never been so sure about anything in my life." He glanced at Kinsley, and their gazes locked. She wanted to look away, but she couldn't. "Well, maybe I've been that sure about one other thing, and she's a big part of the reason that I'm going to say what I have to say. I appreciate this party. I appreciate everybody gathering here to wish me well and to give me such a great sendoff. However, turns out a funny thing happened on the way to the cake table. I realize I won't be moving to New York, after all."

Kinsley was frozen in place, desperately pulling back on the reins of her heart, which was hopefully anticipating a preposterous turn of events that would surely never be.

*So just stop it.*

Audible gasps mixed with surprised murmurs and astonished glances, but Christopher's gaze didn't waver from hers.

"It's always been important to me to be respected and regarded as an intelligent man. But it took a party like this, a gathering of my family and friends and one hell of a party planner—everybody please give Kinsley a round of applause for the wonderful job she did to bring us all together—to clarify some things for me."

Her hand fluttered to her collar. *Oh, why did he do that?*

She finally broke their gaze and glanced around at the people who were clapping for her. She really wished they wouldn't do that.

When they quieted down, Christopher continued. "Today I realize that I love Texas too much to leave. I have just gotten to know my Fortune family, and quite frankly I'm not ready to put that much distance between us. But most of all, there is someone special here I simply can't bear to leave behind."

Kinsley's heart stopped beating for what seemed like an eternity. When it resumed, it picked up double time.

"She has made me a better person. I haven't quite figured out how this happened, and I'm pretty sure I don't deserve her. But I love her. I love her with my entire being, and I can't imagine my life without her."

Kinsley's gasp was audible, surprising even herself. Heat crept up her neck and fanned across her cheeks as every gaze in the place turned to her.

She wasn't sure if she wanted to cry tears

of joy or crawl under the table to escape scrutiny. The tears of joy definitely won out. This unusual proclamation of love certainly wasn't what she had expected when she thought about Christopher declaring his love, but had Christopher Fortune ever done anything by the book?

"I wouldn't blame Kinsley if she killed me right now," Christopher said, hoping he hadn't gone too far with this workplace pronouncement. "So if you see me with a piece of cake smashed in my face, it probably doesn't mean we've gotten married. It probably means she simply smashed that cake in my face, which I suppose I would deserve."

He was relieved when everyone laughed.

He couldn't quite see Kinsley, who had gradually worked her way to the back of the room. Well, he didn't blame her—he probably shouldn't have gotten so carried away. It would serve him right if she told him to take a hike.

He remembered his initial vow to win her over no matter what. He fully expected to have to work harder than he'd ever worked his entire life to get her to commit to him. He'd never looked so forward to a challenge. Speaking of challenges, he still owed everyone the rest of the explanation. He turned back to the group and continued.

"Plenty of folks right here in this room are probably better qualified than I am to open an office in the Big Apple. I was thinking about that while I was standing here enjoying everyone's company. So I offered Emmett, James and Lily a new proposal for the Fortune Foundation, but this one hits a little closer to home. With their blessing, I will be opening a satellite office of the Foundation in Horseback Hollow, with an anti-bullying/GET INVOLVED initiative. I will split time between Horseback Hollow and Red Rock. So, I'm sorry to say that you haven't gotten rid of me yet."

As his family and coworkers applauded this news, Christopher scanned the room for Kinsley, wanting to gauge her reaction, but he didn't see her. He wanted to go find her, but people approached and started the whole process all over again of shaking his hand, slapping him on the back and congratulating him—on the satellite office and on falling in love with a wonderful woman. They all seemed genuinely pleased for him. It was very moving, but he was starting to get a little anxious over Kinsley's absence.

Had she left?

He wouldn't blame her if she'd walked out. But if she had, he would fix it.

If it was the last thing he did, he would fix things between them.

He excused himself again from the knot of well-wishers and went to look for her.

He found her in the reception area standing quietly gazing out the window. It was a similar view as from his office, the one that had captivated him from the start. He'd thought the south Texas landscape couldn't look more beautiful. But he'd never seen it as a backdrop to Kinsley.

"I meant what I said in there," he said. "I'm in love with you. I may have changed my mind about the job, but I'm not going to change my mind about you. All I need to know is do I even stand a chance after all I've put you through?"

She turned and met his gaze. Her beautiful eyes were brimming with tears. In that instant he knew everything was going to be okay.

He walked over to her, pulled her into his arms and reached up and brushed a tear off her cheek.

"Don't worry," she said. "They're happy tears. I love you, too."

* * *

Kinsley was never so happy to leave a party—even one she'd planned. But she knew the two of them would have a much better time at the after party—in Christopher's bed.

With him, she was home, even amid the partially packed boxes that would now need to be unpacked. Yes, she was more than happy to help him with this task. It was the packing and the goodbyes she couldn't bear.

They spent a long, luxurious evening making love and snuggling and making love and snuggling. She couldn't tell if they were making up for lost time or living in the moment, but it didn't matter. They didn't need to define it. They already had when they had exchanged those three precious words that even twelve hours ago she feared she would never hear cross his lips.

If she had learned one thing about Christopher it was that when he said something he meant it. His word was golden, and Kinsley basked in the glow of it as he held her.

She splayed her hand across his chest, reveling in the downy-soft feel of his chest hair.

"So, speaking of being the last to know..." she said.

He pulled her closer, as if he were afraid she would get away.

"Oh, hell…here we go." He smiled and pretended to roll his eyes before he kissed her soundly. "I knew there would be hell to pay for what I did. May I make it up to you…again? Because I am perfectly willing to make love to you until you fully understand just how much I love you."

He shifted her to the side and then rolled on top of her.

"Oh, you have no idea how much trouble you are in, mister." She kissed his neck and then nipped at his earlobe as he nudged her legs apart and entered her again.

After they were spent and breathless, she managed to catch her breath. "As I was saying, I had to hear through the grapevine that you called your father. And that the two of you had a good talk."

He did a double-take. "Oh, yeah? Who is spreading such rumors?"

"I'm not telling."

He grinned at her slyly. "I thought we promised that there would be no secrets between us. Am I going to have to assign you penance?"

"Please do. I could be a very happy woman doing atonement with you." She traced his lips with her index finger, getting momentarily lost in the mix of masculine strength and male beauty that was Christopher.

She swallowed around a lump of love and gratitude that had settled in her throat.

Or maybe it was her heart that was so full it was spilling over. Whatever the case, she never wanted it to go away. She wanted it to keep bubbling up like a fountain.

She settled into the crook of his arm and rested her head in that place on his shoulder that seemed to be made just for her.

"Actually, it's not a rumor," he said. "I did call my dad. Deke said to tell you hello."

"Really?" she asked.

"No, but I do want to take you home to Horseback Hollow so that you can meet him and my mother. I know she'll love you. They will all love you. Maybe not quite as much as I do, but I don't know that that's humanly possible. But I digress.

"The call went great. Better than great. I underestimated my father. I learned that he and I are two different men, but that's okay. We have finally come to the point where we accept that and respect each other for who we are."

"I'm so glad," Kinsley said.

Gently, he rubbed her back in a slow, rhythmic motion that was almost hypnotizing. She couldn't remember the last time she had been this relaxed.

"I might not have called him—or at least not so soon—if not for you. Thank you for that. Thank you for always seeing the best in me."

"Well, not *always*— Remember, you still have a lot of penance before you're completely redeemed. But I can assure you that I do love what I see."

They were quiet for a moment. The air-conditioning clicked on. Somewhere out in the world, outside the snug cocoon that had become their universe, a car door shut and a dog barked.

"So, who do you look like—your mom or your dad?"

"Everyone says I take after my dad. In looks and personality. My brothers say that's why Deke and I butt heads so often. That we're too much alike."

"I'd love to see a picture of him sometime. He must be a good-looking guy."

Christopher stretched. "My mama thinks so. She's stuck with him for forty years. Can you believe they've been married that long?"

"I think that's wonderful."

"Maybe that gives you a little hope for me.

I don't commit easily, but once I do, I'm sort of like gum on your shoe."

"That's *so* romantic."

They laughed. She loved the way they didn't take themselves too seriously.

"At least I think I'll be the gum on your shoe. I've never loved someone enough to be their gum."

"Wow. How did I get so lucky?"

They laughed again, and when they stopped, she lost herself in his sigh of contentment.

"So, now, tell me again, how many brothers and sisters do you have?"

"I'm one of seven."

"Holy cow. Your poor mother."

"Nah, Mama loved her children. There are two girls and five boys, including me. A handful."

"Sounds like your mother should be canonized."

"Yup, pretty much. Wait—" he said sitting up suddenly. "I want to show you something."

Kinsley enjoyed watching him walk from the bed to the bedroom door.

"What a fine specimen you are, Mr. Fortune."

When he returned he was holding a photo

album. The one she remembered seeing in his car that night they went to Mendoza's.

The night everything started.

"What's that?" she asked as he climbed back into bed beside her.

"It's a photo album my mother sent me to remind me of where I came from."

"And you're letting me look now? Remember that night before we went to Mendoza's? I thought you were going to smack my hand away from it."

He looked at her solemnly, momentarily sobering. "Besides loving you for the rest of your life, the other thing I can promise you is that I will never, ever raise a hand to you."

She inhaled sharply and nodded.

In that moment, she sensed that her mother was with her. That her mother, the angel, had quite possibly sent Christopher to watch over her. The kind of man she should have, rather than the kind of bad example her father had set.

*Everything is going to be all right, Mom. Everything is fine now.*

"Here," said Christopher. "Look at this picture. Here's my dad when he was about my age."

Wrapped in the sheet, Kinsley scooted up and sat next to Christopher on the bed.

She studied the picture, loving this new window into her love's world. "Wow, you do look like him."

"My dad's name is Jones. Deke Jones. I'm going to start using Jones in my name again. How would you feel about being part of the Fortune Jones family?"

"Hmm… Kinsley Aaron Fortune Jones," she said. "That's a mouthful. But it sounds like poetry to me."

When Christopher leaned in and kissed her. She knew that she was home, that she had finally found her family at last.

\* \* \* \* \*

# Get 4 FREE REWARDS!

## We'll send you 2 FREE Books plus 2 FREE Mystery Gifts.

**Harlequin® Special Edition** books feature heroines finding the balance between their work life and personal life on the way to finding true love.

FREE Value Over $20

---

**YES!** Please send me 2 FREE Harlequin® Special Edition novels and my 2 FREE gifts (gifts are worth about $10 retail). After receiving them, if I don't wish to receive any more books, I can return the shipping statement marked "cancel." If I don't cancel, I will receive 6 brand-new novels every month and be billed just $4.99 per book in the U.S. or $5.74 per book in Canada. That's a savings of at least 12% off the cover price! It's quite a bargain! Shipping and handling is just 50¢ per book in the U.S. and 75¢ per book in Canada.* I understand that accepting the 2 free books and gifts places me under no obligation to buy anything. I can always return a shipment and cancel at any time. The free books and gifts are mine to keep no matter what I decide.

235/335 HDN GMY2

Name (please print)

Address                                                                              Apt. #

City                              State/Province                    Zip/Postal Code

### Mail to the **Reader Service:**
IN U.S.A.: P.O. Box 1341, Buffalo, NY 14240-8531
IN CANADA: P.O. Box 603, Fort Erie, Ontario L2A 5X3

Want to try 2 free books from another series! Call 1-800-873-8635 or visit www.ReaderService.com.

*Terms and prices subject to change without notice. Prices do not include sales taxes, which will be charged (if applicable) based on your state or country of residence. Canadian residents will be charged applicable taxes. Offer not valid in Quebec. This offer is limited to one order per household. Books received may not be as shown. Not valid for current subscribers to Harlequin® Special Edition books. All orders subject to approval. Credit or debit balances in a customer's account(s) may be offset by any other outstanding balance owed by or to the customer. Please allow 4 to 6 weeks for delivery. Offer available while quantities last.

**Your Privacy**—The Reader Service is committed to protecting your privacy. Our Privacy Policy is available online at www.ReaderService.com or upon request from the Reader Service. We make a portion of our mailing list available to reputable third parties that offer products we believe may interest you. If you prefer that we not exchange your name with third parties, or if you wish to clarify or modify your communication preferences, please visit us at www.ReaderService.com/consumerchoice or write to us at Reader Service Preference Service, P.O. Box 9062, Buffalo, NY 14240-9062. Include your complete name and address.

HSE19R

# Get 4 FREE REWARDS!

### We'll send you 2 FREE Books <u>plus</u> 2 FREE Mystery Gifts.

**Harlequin® Romance Larger-Print** books feature uplifting escapes that will warm your heart with the ultimate feel-good tales.

FREE
Value Over
**$20**

---

**YES!** Please send me 2 FREE Harlequin® Romance Larger-Print novels and my 2 FREE gifts (gifts are worth about $10 retail). After receiving them, if I don't wish to receive any more books, I can return the shipping statement marked "cancel." If I don't cancel, I will receive 4 brand-new novels every month and be billed just $5.34 per book in the U.S. or $5.74 per book in Canada. That's a savings of at least 15% off the cover price! It's quite a bargain! Shipping and handling is just 50¢ per book in the U.S. and 75¢ per book in Canada.* I understand that accepting the 2 free books and gifts places me under no obligation to buy anything. I can always return a shipment and cancel at any time. The free books and gifts are mine to keep no matter what I decide.

119/319 HDN GMYY

Name (please print)

Address                                                                 Apt. #

City                              State/Province                        Zip/Postal Code

> ### Mail to the **Reader Service:**
> **IN U.S.A.:** P.O. Box 1341, Buffalo, NY 14240-8531
> **IN CANADA:** P.O. Box 603, Fort Erie, Ontario L2A 5X3

Want to try 2 free books from another series? Call 1-800-873-8635 or visit www.ReaderService.com.

*Terms and prices subject to change without notice. Prices do not include sales taxes, which will be charged (if applicable) based on your state or country of residence. Canadian residents will be charged applicable taxes. Offer not valid in Quebec. This offer is limited to one order per household. Books received may not be as shown. Not valid for current subscribers to Harlequin Romance Larger-Print books. All orders subject to approval. Credit or debit balances in a customer's account(s) may be offset by any other outstanding balance owed by or to the customer. Please allow 4 to 6 weeks for delivery. Offer available while quantities last.

**Your Privacy**—The Reader Service is committed to protecting your privacy. Our Privacy Policy is available online at www.ReaderService.com or upon request from the Reader Service. We make a portion of our mailing list available to reputable third parties that offer products we believe may interest you. If you prefer that we not exchange your name with third parties, or if you wish to clarify or modify your communication preferences, please visit us at www.ReaderService.com/consumerchoice or write to us at Reader Service Preference Service, P.O. Box 9062, Buffalo, NY 14240-9062. Include your complete name and address.

HRLP19R

# Get 4 FREE REWARDS!

## We'll send you 2 FREE Books plus 2 FREE Mystery Gifts.

FREE
Value Over
$20

Both the **Romance** and **Suspense** collections feature compelling novels written by many of today's best-selling authors.

**YES!** Please send me 2 FREE novels from the Essential Romance or Essential Suspense Collection and my 2 FREE gifts (gifts are worth about $10 retail). After receiving them, if I don't wish to receive any more books, I can return the shipping statement marked "cancel." If I don't cancel, I will receive 4 brand-new novels every month and be billed just $6.74 each in the U.S. or $7.24 each in Canada. That's a savings of at least 16% off the cover price. It's quite a bargain! Shipping and handling is just 50¢ per book in the U.S. and 75¢ per book in Canada.* I understand that accepting the 2 free books and gifts places me under no obligation to buy anything. I can always return a shipment and cancel at any time. The free books and gifts are mine to keep no matter what I decide.

Choose one: ☐ **Essential Romance**
(194/394 MDN GMY7)

☐ **Essential Suspense**
(191/391 MDN GMY7)

Name (please print)

Address                                                                                        Apt. #

City                                          State/Province                          Zip/Postal Code

### Mail to the **Reader Service**:
**IN U.S.A.:** P.O. Box 1341, Buffalo, NY 14240-8531
**IN CANADA:** P.O. Box 603, Fort Erie, Ontario L2A 5X3

Want to try 2 free books from another series? Call 1-800-873-8635 or visit www.ReaderService.com.

*Terms and prices subject to change without notice. Prices do not include sales taxes, which will be charged (if applicable) based on your state or country of residence. Canadian residents will be charged applicable taxes. Offer not valid in Quebec. This offer is limited to one order per household. Books received may not be as shown. Not valid for current subscribers to the Essential Romance or Essential Suspense Collection. All orders subject to approval. Credit or debit balances in a customer's account(s) may be offset by any other outstanding balance owed by or to the customer. Please allow 4 to 6 weeks for delivery. Offer available while quantities last.

**Your Privacy**—The Reader Service is committed to protecting your privacy. Our Privacy Policy is available online at www.ReaderService.com or upon request from the Reader Service. We make a portion of our mailing list available to reputable third parties that offer products we believe may interest you. If you prefer that we not exchange your name with third parties, or if you wish to clarify or modify your communication preferences, please visit us at www.ReaderService.com/consumerschoice or write to us at Reader Service Preference Service, P.O. Box 9062, Buffalo, NY 14240-9062. Include your complete name and address.

STRS19R

# Get 4 FREE REWARDS!

### We'll send you 2 FREE Books
### plus 2 FREE Mystery Gifts.

**Harlequin® Heartwarming™ Larger-Print** books feature traditional values of home, family, community and—most of all—love.

FREE
Value Over
$20

**YES!** Please send me 2 FREE Harlequin® Heartwarming™ Larger-Print novels and my 2 FREE mystery gifts (gifts worth about $10 retail). After receiving them, if I don't wish to receive any more books, I can return the shipping statement marked "cancel." If I don't cancel, I will receive 4 brand-new larger-print novels every month and be billed just $5.49 per book in the U.S. or $6.24 per book in Canada. That's a savings of at least 19% off the cover price. It's quite a bargain! Shipping and handling is just 50¢ per book in the U.S. and 75¢ per book in Canada.* I understand that accepting the 2 free books and gifts places me under no obligation to buy anything. I can always return a shipment and cancel at any time. The free books and gifts are mine to keep no matter what I decide.

161/361 IDN GMY3

Name (please print)

Address                                                                                   Apt. #

City                                          State/Province                        Zip/Postal Code

### Mail to the **Reader Service:**
**IN U.S.A.:** P.O. Box 1341, Buffalo, NY 14240-8531
**IN CANADA:** P.O. Box 603, Fort Erie, Ontario L2A 5X3

Want to try 2 free books from another series? Call 1-800-873-8635 or visit www.ReaderService.com.

*Terms and prices subject to change without notice. Prices do not include sales taxes, which will be charged (if applicable) based on your state or country of residence. Canadian residents will be charged applicable taxes. Offer not valid in Quebec. This offer is limited to one order per household. Books received may not be as shown. Not valid for current subscribers to Harlequin Heartwarming Larger-Print books. All orders subject to approval. Credit or debit balances in a customer's account(s) may be offset by any other outstanding balance owed by or to the customer. Please allow 4 to 6 weeks for delivery. Offer available while quantities last.

**Your Privacy**—The Reader Service is committed to protecting your privacy. Our Privacy Policy is available online at www.ReaderService.com or upon request from the Reader Service. We make a portion of our mailing list available to reputable third parties that offer products we believe may interest you. If you prefer that we not exchange your name with third parties, or if you wish to clarify or modify your communication preferences, please visit us at www.ReaderService.com/consumerschoice or write to us at Reader Service Preference Service, P.O. Box 9062, Buffalo, NY 14240-9062. Include your complete name and address.

HW19R

# READERSERVICE.COM

## Manage your account online!

- Review your order history
- Manage your payments
- Update your address

*We've designed the*
*Reader Service website*
*just for you.*

## Enjoy all the features!

- Discover new series available to you, and read excerpts from any series.
- Respond to mailings and special monthly offers.
- Browse the Bonus Bucks catalog and online-only exculsives.
- Share your feedback.

*Visit us at:*
# ReaderService.com

RS16R